What Bool
Women in (
and Journ

MW00883506

Secrets of the Pastor's Wife

"In *Secrets of the Pastor's Wife*, Claypool delicately and beautifully shares a fictional story about the power of forgiveness. Having been an Inspirational Book Club leader, I believe this novel would be an incredible fit for discussion, because it covers so many important issues. It has the ability to allow readers to rediscover the hurt, regret, and shame they may still carry from their past and to experience healing and restoration. It will challenge them to believe they are never too far gone to receive God's forgiveness and mercy."

Mandy Woodward, Former Discussion Leader
Just a Little Inspiration Book Club
Milton-Union Public Library - West Milton, Ohio

"This book was a compelling and easy read, which is perfect for busy women. I could readily relate to the pastor's wife who guarded her heart, wearing a mask of protection, with the constant fear of being exposed. We are all broken, and being able to trust and be vulnerable is difficult. Yet our secrets and skeletons can hold us captive and steal our joy. This story shows the unraveling of a tangled web, but ultimately hope and healing replace pain and shame."

Rebecca Carter, Stephen Minister/GriefShare Coordinator
Clearwater, Florida

"Secrets of the Pastor's Wife is Christina Ryan Claypool's first foray into fiction. It should not be her last. Dare we suggest that perhaps other residents of Maple Grove have secrets to reveal? We'd look forward to a return visit."

Patricia Ann Speelman, Local Life Editor
Sidney (Ohio) Daily News

"Secrets of the Pastor's Wife is a great reminder that all of us have issues/secrets from our past to deal with, and that we need help dealing with this baggage. After being a pastor's wife for almost four decades and then pastoring with my husband for the past 25 years, I know firsthand how a minister's spouse might feel like they don't have anyone with whom to share their struggles. But they should be encouraged by this writing to find that individual who they can reach out to for prayer and for greater healing in their lives."

Pastor Sue Bowers, Co-Pastor/pastor's wife
Grace Fellowship International Church
Erie, Pennsylvania

Secrets
OF THE *PASTOR'S* *Wife*

CHRISTINA RYAN CLAYPOOL

WESTBOW
PRESS®
A DIVISION OF THOMAS NELSON
& ZONDERVAN

Cover artwork by Marge Brandt
Author photo by Mike Ullery

This is a work of fiction. All of the characters, names, incidents,
organizations, and dialogue in this novel are either the products
of the author's imagination or are used fictitiously.

WestBow Press books may be ordered through booksellers or by contacting:

WestBow Press
A Division of Thomas Nelson & Zondervan
1663 Liberty Drive
Bloomington, IN 47403
www.westbowpress.com
1 (866) 928-1240

ISBN: 978-1-9736-0135-7 (sc)
ISBN: 978-1-9736-0134-0 (e)

Library of Congress Control Number: 2017913608

Print information available on the last page.

WestBow Press rev. date: 08/13/2018

Dedicated to Lauren

You will be forever in my
heart until we meet again

I love you always,
Aunt Christina

Contents

Acknowledgments...ix

Chapter 1:   The Pastor's Parsonage.......................................1
Chapter 2:   Katie's Story 14
Chapter 3:   Getting to Know Each Other 29
Chapter 4:   A Family's Secret 40
Chapter 5:   Broken Vow..58
Chapter 6:   A Gatsby Look-Alike..72
Chapter 7:   A Tragic Tale of Innocence Lost....................83
Chapter 8:   A Match Made in Heaven 94
Chapter 9:   The Beginning of Forgiveness......................107
Chapter 10: The Keeper of All Secrets 119
Book Club or Bible Study Discussion Questions.................139

Bonus Short Story "Not Just Another Casserole Lady".....145
Discussion Questions 154

Christina Ryan Claypool genuinely appreciates learning the stories of readers who have been impacted in some way by *Secrets of the Pastor's Wife.* To contact Christina with your story, regarding a speaking engagement, or for more information about other available products visit her website at: www.christinaryanclaypool.com

She blogs at:
www.christinaryanclaypool.com/blog1

Connect with her through Facebook or Twitter

Email christina@christinaryanclaypool.com
or write to her US Postal Service:

Christina Ryan Claypool
New Creations
P.O. Box 711
Tipp City, OH 45371

Acknowledgments

Some years ago, while working as a TV reporter, I interviewed award-winning singer/songwriter Kathy Troccoli. Unknowingly, this humble Christian celebrity taught me a valuable lesson that is the basis for this book.

"Secrets make you sick," is what she said with great compassion referring to the painful issues we sometimes conceal, affecting multitudes of the hidden brokenhearted among us. From that point on, I became even more passionate about the spiritual importance of sharing past hurts to find emotional wholeness. So thanks, Ms. Troccoli, for setting me on a path to see myself and others ultimately set free.

Heartfelt appreciation to Mike Lackey, Patti Speelman, and Kate Johnsen, three caring editors who assisted me when I got stuck, and encouraged me when I doubted myself. I couldn't have done it without you. Cindy Sproles, your cover advice, and Mike Ullery (photo) were true gifts!

My deepest gratitude to award-winning artist Marge Brandt for her lovely watercolor creation on the cover. Marge is in her late eighties, but she graciously agreed to lend her talents to this project, the same way she did more than two decades ago when she painted my first book cover.

Marital kudos to love of my life, Larry Claypool, for putting up with my quirky writer ways and for donating his talented editing skills whenever I got in a pinch. Zach Ryan, forever thanks for loving me. Despite my being a self-admitted helicopter mom, you grew up to be a remarkable adult.

To my dear friend, Carol Foulkes, your long-ago lesson about "the little boy who lives inside of every man" has proven priceless. Thanks for sharing your wisdom with me, so I could share it with others.

To you, the readers of this book, thank you from the bottom of my heart for purchasing and investing your precious time to read *Secrets of the Pastor's Wife.* I pray God blesses you with a new sense of freedom, compassion, and a big dose of His unconditional love.

Special thanks to the folks who reside in one of the real Maple Grove, Ohio's. I appreciate you letting me borrow the name. My Maple Grove and its inhabitants are fictional and any resemblance to actual persons or places is purely coincidental.

Most of all, praise, honor, and glory, to God who is the Keeper of all secrets, and who loves and forgives us no matter how dark and messy our past might be.

Chapter 1
The Pastor's Parsonage

WHEN CASSANDRA MARTIN first moved to Maple Grove, the silence in the middle of the night seemed eerie. The only sounds were the occasional hum of a slow moving automobile or the rustling wind blowing through the maple trees that line the main street of the village.

Main Street. This is where Cassie lives in a little white house built just after World War II. It is surrounded by red tulips in the spring and yellow roses in the summer. Despite the flowers, the well-cared-for home is rather stark and common-looking. Of course, a white picket fence encloses it, which lends a feeling of privacy.

It is the perfect pastor's parsonage, or so the people of Maple Avenue Community Church think. On the other hand, the majestic brick church building that sits next to the house on the corner of Main Street and Maple Avenue is adorned with exquisite multi-colored stained-glass windows and hand-carved woodwork. It is anything but plain.

Initially, the village's fascination with maple trees both

1

amused and irritated Cassie. On her first day there, their new neighbor, Pauline Alana, welcomed her with a hot apple pie while sharing the story of the red maple. With the aroma of the freshly baked pie filling the parsonage, she felt compelled to listen politely to her neighbor's tree lesson.

"There are many varieties of maples, with the red, silver, and sugar maple being common throughout Ohio," explained Pauline, a forty-something registered nurse by profession. "The red maple is known for the crimson autumn foliage that our village of about 3,500 residents became famous for. During the fall, tourists drive from all over just to see the breathtaking panorama of blazing red leaves. Mrs. Martin, you're going to love the fall here...."

"Please, call me Cassie. All my friends do," interrupted the exhausted pastor's wife. But what Cassie Martin was thinking was, *What I would really love is for you to leave, so I can unpack some more boxes.* She was thankful Pauline couldn't read her mind, since a minister's spouse wasn't ever supposed to be unkind, but she was only human.

Besides, the poor pastor's wife had experienced a terrible shock just minutes earlier. She'd been going through a box of books when she'd happened to pick up her high school copy of the famous novel, *The Great Gatsby.* Feeling nostalgic, she'd opened it, and an old photograph fell to the floor. She had no idea she had kept it.

Instantly, she'd been flooded with agonizing memories that brought tears to her eyes. Compulsively, she'd torn the photo into tiny pieces, then thrown them in the trash, making sure they were at the bottom. Cassie had been in the bathroom staring blankly into the mirror when she'd heard the knock.

She hadn't had time to compose herself, but she'd thought she had better answer it. Quickly, Cassie dabbed at her eyes with some toilet paper ripped from the roll that the church ladies had graciously placed in the bathroom. She'd taken a deep breath and headed for her new front door, opening it to a smiling stranger with a heavenly-smelling pie in her hand.

It was uncharacteristic for Cassie Martin not to be welcoming and compassionate with people. This was her strength in ministry, the strength her husband could count on. Even though she was shy, few folks knew it, because the attractive brunette would take great effort to reach out to those who were hurting. If someone lost a family member, struggled with an illness, or dealt with any kind of heartbreak, Cassie always tried to comfort them. The way she did this was by taking the time to listen.

Cassie wouldn't have reacted so negatively to Pauline, but instead of asking if she could help with the unpacking, her new neighbor had plopped down in the only available chair and settled in for a visit. A weary Cassie sensed that her history lesson had just started, and she was both tired and hungry from moving all day. Added to that was the distress of being haunted by old secrets that never seemed to go away, no matter how many times she moved.

"I'm sorry, what were you saying?" Cassie managed to pull herself together. "Please, forgive me. I'm a bit tired."

3

Instead of picking up on the exhausted woman's subtle hint, Pauline forged ahead. "I totally understand. I was talking about the maple trees, Cassie. Besides naming the town, the church, the school, and a street after the tree, there is also the Maple Grove Inn, the Maple Crest Restaurant, and the Maple View Theatre." Without taking a breath, she continued, "The Maple Grove Inn isn't a resort hotel, but rather an old Victorian house with three upper bedrooms that are rented out by the night, week, or month." Pauline chuckled to herself. "Actually, there are two bedrooms available, as Billy Joe Horton, the town drunk, lives in one of the rooms year-round. Jolene Sanders and her teenage daughter, Missy, stay in another bedroom when her husband acts up. Some say the poor man has a heroin habit. But, I'm getting ahead of myself." Pauline glanced at Cassie with a conspiratorial look that said, *Would you like me to tell you more about the Sanders family?*

She had hit a nerve. Cassie hated gossip, because the pastor's wife knew what it felt like to be the one gossiped about. Acting naïve, she quickly changed the subject and seemed sincere when she asked Pauline to tell her more of the town history.

"Oh, sure," said Pauline, who prided herself on being an expert on just about everything. "The Maple View Theatre was built at the turn of the century, when traveling vaudeville shows performed in the area. Old timers say that Will Rogers, a famous comedian and trick roper, once headlined there."

Pauline waited to see if Cassie was impressed by this bit of historical information.

Since she wasn't, Pauline admitted, "Because it happened more than a century ago, no one knows for sure if the story is true. Well, anyway...by the 1930s, when movies had replaced vaudeville, the building was renovated to serve as a movie theater. The smell of hot buttered popcorn greeted Maple Grove residents and local farmers as they handed over their hard-earned cash to pay for admittance to the latest film."

Cassie smiled politely while wondering, *When is she ever going to leave? John will be home soon, and I have no idea what we are going to do for supper.*

"But last year, the theater's owners went bankrupt, and the need for expensive repairs has caused the once-magnificent structure to sit vacant." Pauline seemed unaware of Cassie's impatience. "Sadly, the dilapidated building closed for good after serving the community for over a century."

In her current state of exhaustion, this local history was about as interesting to Cassie Martin as the fact that the village was named after the red maple tree. But, she was the new pastor's wife, and she didn't want to offend Pauline. *Everyone knows that a good pastor's wife is supposed to smooth ruffled feathers, not be the one ruffling them.*

Finally, her next-door neighbor left her to her boxes and thoughts about what she could rustle up for supper. She did leave behind the delicious apple pie, which convinced Cassie that she probably had a good heart but bad timing.

This first encounter with Pauline happened about a year

ago, when Cassie's husband accepted the senior pastorate at Maple Avenue Community Church. Everyone who is anyone—not just in Maple Grove, but in the entire county—goes to M.A.C. Church. More than 700 folks regularly attend Sunday worship, with an additional 600 listing themselves on the membership roll. The majority of those who never show up are either housebound, in a nursing home, or sending their tithes in to soothe their consciences' need to belong to a fellowship.

The church sanctuary has the original stained-glass windows, which gloriously depict scenes of Jesus' life. The multi-colored creations reflect the sunlight onto the white walls of the remodeled sanctuary that is capable of seating almost 600, since the pews were replaced with padded chairs. Those chairs are most likely the reason a former pastor resigned, but that's another story. Even if there were enough seating, two services would be necessary, because the contemporary crowd doesn't mix well with the traditional congregation.

That's why at 9:00 a.m. on Sunday morning, Maple Avenue Community Church resembles most traditional denominations nationwide. There's an organist, hymns, and a small choir dressed in robes for special occasions. With 300 in attendance, mostly silver-haired seniors outfitted in their Sunday best, the pastor preaches in a suit and tie for exactly twenty minutes. But at 11:00 a.m., the sanctuary fills with Praise and Worship music from guitars and driving drums, and a mostly younger, jean-clad crowd of 400-plus. The same pastor exchanges his suit pants for jeans, loses the tie, and suddenly he is expected to become relevant and cutting-edge.

The church board reads like a "Who's Who" in the village, including local car dealer Jay Briggs, village librarian Sally Lewis, wealthy farmer "old" Ed Hardy Sr., accountant "young" Ed Hardy Jr., and postmistress Rita McCoy. Miss McCoy's nickname is "Rita Rules." People only use this name when they talk about her behind her back, because Rita is an obsessive stickler for postal regulations.

Years ago, Cassie gave up trying to win the affection of church board members, since she knew how fickle their allegiance could be—especially if her husband found himself on the wrong side of an issue. What's more, in the little towns where they had served, everyone was related, and blood really is thicker than water.

In the beginning, it had hurt her deeply when she developed a friendship, only to have it severed because of a difference in opinion. It was rarely over major spiritual issues, but more like whether to paint or wallpaper the walls in the sanctuary, who should fund the youth group's Missions trip, or how much the church secretary should make in her weekly salary. Cassie hated that she had such a jaded attitude, especially in Maple Grove, where the board seemed genuinely concerned about meeting the needs of the new minister and his wife.

"They did everything possible to make the transition easy for us," Cassie told her husband one evening over supper. "Still, I'm not sure if I should start a garden or unpack my good china dishes, because we both know the Maple Avenue congregation has a recent history of not keeping a pastor very long." The couple had served at several other churches like this, and she protected her heart by not becoming too attached to her surroundings.

"But it's challenging not to become attached to Maple Grove, since the rustic landscape, quaint village and outgoing townspeople have a way of winning a newcomer's heart," Pastor John confessed as he took a bite of the homemade German chocolate cake that one of the church's widows, 78-year-old Ethel Palmer, had dropped off as a housewarming present.

The delicious cake didn't change the fact that the pastor's wife had moved half a dozen times in the fifteen years since she and John had married following his graduation from seminary. It wasn't that they weren't liked, but just the opposite. Each relocation had included a promotion to either a larger church or greater financial stability.

The couple always lived in a parsonage, a house that belonged to the church they were serving. Sometimes, the churches were generous and thoughtful, and their home was more than modest. On other occasions, John and Cassie were provided with a dwelling that had faded wallpaper, a leaky roof, or a running toilet which had been neglected when a congregation was less than considerate of the pastor's family. Thankfully, in Maple Grove the couple was greeted with freshly painted walls, brand-new appliances, and just-cleaned carpet throughout the three-bedroom A-frame house.

"A church offering a home to live in as part of the salary compensation is becoming somewhat of a rarity, since most now offer a housing allowance," John Martin explained to his devoted spouse early in their marriage. "That's why I search for these assignments, because in rural areas, a good rental can be hard to find, and it would be unwise to buy a house until we are sure we will be putting down roots for good."

"I agree, John. Buying a house could financially bankrupt us, if we had to move and were unable to resell." Cassie didn't complain about living in a parsonage, because she understood how capricious a congregation's allegiance to its minister could be. Instead each time the Martins moved to a new assignment, Cassie used the creative ability that she had been born with to transform an often austere residence into a cozy homestead. Pastor John marveled at this artistic gift.

"I'm in awe of your talent to take whatever residence a church provides for us and to make something beautiful out of it, no matter the condition," he once remarked when his artistic spouse brightened faded mint green kitchen walls with fresh pale yellow paint, along with touching up the chipped white cabinets in a parsonage that hadn't been remodeled since the 1960s. "You bought a little paint and added a lot of elbow grease, and the kitchen looks like one of those makeovers on TV," he said with admiration when she finished the project. With Cassie's flair for decorating, it didn't take much to make the updated Maple Grove parsonage inviting.

Cassie had studied fine arts at the prestigious University

of the Arts located in a suburb of Philadelphia almost two decades ago. Although she isn't a famous artist like Van Gogh or Picasso, occasionally she sells paintings through one of the independent galleries that stock her work or through participating in a community art show. She also looks for commercial freelance art jobs to supplement the family budget, but assignments are scarce.

She tries to be grateful, because she loves her husband and immensely enjoys painting. Anyway, she would never want to hurt him with the truth. *"I long to have a home that I could call my own. Just once, I would like to be the one to decide what color of carpet to buy or whether my house siding should be in white or blue. I'm over 40, and I've never even purchased a new appliance like a refrigerator or washing machine. It would be such a blessing to have that freedom."* She had written these words in her prayer journal. She also admitted, *"I feel guilty for wanting an earthly possession like a house so badly, but as I age, my nesting desire seems to grow stronger. I also wish we had the financial stability that owning equity in a home could provide."*

As for stability, Pastor John Martin is as dependable a man as God ever created. On Sunday mornings, sitting on the front row listening to John preach, Cassie still feels blessed that she was the girl he chose to marry. He isn't handsome by any stretch of the imagination. The 40-year-old pastor is 5'10", and due to the fact that he enjoys eating, he weighs over 200 pounds. How much over, he never shares.

The best word to describe John Martin is stocky. His head

of thick blond hair that Cassie enjoyed running her fingers through in their early years of marriage has been replaced by a shiny head that is bald. All that remains is a fringe of sparse, grayish blond that becomes wet with perspiration whenever he exerts himself in any way. Pastor John has etched facial features that make him look aristocratic, and his intense blue eyes are so sensitive that they seem to burrow their way into a wounded person's soul.

John's physical appearance doesn't matter. "I think my husband is the most precious gift God has ever given me," declared his adoring mate on one occasion. "Although like every marriage, there are moments when his dirty socks lying on the living room floor or his piles of books and papers annoy me." Cassie smiled remembering an argument about this subject not long after their honeymoon. "Through the years, Pastor John has tried to pick his things up, understanding it's important to me, but sometimes, when he's tired or rushed, he forgets. I attempt to be merciful when this happens, unlike the nagging wife mentioned in Proverbs, because who wants to be that kind of woman?

"I'm a realist, and believe that only God Himself could have provided such a jewel for me. We met when I was 25, and John had just turned 24. Even though I was young, I was almost convinced that there was no longer a 'Mr. Right' for me. I was afraid that my youthful rebellion might have cost me this opportunity," Cassie confided. She wasn't naïve. She knew with her looks, she could have landed a lot of men. She just wasn't sure that she could still get a man of integrity like her John.

She told me all this once, while she was having coffee in the coffeehouse that I opened in Maple Grove the year before John and Cassie moved here. My name is Katherine Montague, but all my friends call me Katie. My coffee shop is Katie's Coffee Corner. There's always a cup of steaming-hot coffee waiting for everyone who walks in the carved oak and glass front door. Cassie Martin likes sugar-free caramel lattes and flavored coffee. Her eyes lit up the first time she stopped in when she found out that we brew four special flavors a day.

The pastor's wife was wearing a long, flowing peasant dress that afternoon, but the cotton fabric couldn't hide the fact that she could have been a model. Her thick brunette hair cascaded down the middle of her back. Her hazel eyes were mesmerizing, but there was a sadness that haunted them, a sadness I could never quite put my finger on, until I knew the whole story.

Cassie attributes her youthful physique to watching her diet and years of Pilates classes. By the time I met her, she was starting to show her age just a little bit. There were crow's feet beginning to form at the sides of her eyes, and a deep line framed each side of her mouth—the kind of tell-tale wrinkles most women get in their early forties. Cassie Martin had celebrated her 41st birthday the week she moved to Maple Grove.

As for me, I'm in my mid-sixties, so there are few folks

here whose lives haven't intersected with mine in some way. Most of my customers know me, because I have always lived in Maple Grove. God gave me wonderful parents in Marvin and Agnes Calloway, who both died more than a decade ago, just a few months apart. I was also blessed with a loving husband named Jacob Montague, who farmed his family's land just outside of town for four decades. But, after more than 40 years of being married to the best man in the whole world, I lost my beloved Jake a couple of years back. That's why I decided to open Katie's Coffee Corner.

Honestly, I was lonely. For some reason, Jake and I couldn't ever have children. That's one thing Cassie and I have in common. When Jake and I were first married, we tried. We even went to doctors, but back then they didn't have too many remedies to help an infertile couple.

As for Cassie, she found out a couple years before she met John that she probably wouldn't be able to have a child either. But I'm getting ahead of myself. Before I tell you Cassie's story, I have to tell you a little of mine.

Chapter 2
Katie's Story

JAKE AND I never did find out whose "fault" it was that we couldn't have children. We didn't care, since we figured if the good Lord wanted us to have babies, eventually things would work out. But things never did, at least not in that department.

Jake was tall and lanky in an athletic sort of way. He had a full head of dark hair, which turned silver when he was in his fifties. It was the kind of hair that men who make commercials for hair products have: full and wavy, and so healthy-looking it glistened in the sunlight.

As for me, when I was young, people said I looked like the classic All-American girl. With blonde hair and blue eyes, my 5'7" frame never seemed to carry more than 120 pounds, no matter how much of Lizzie's barbeque chicken or pecan pie I ate.

To explain, when I was only five, my mother almost died in a car accident just a year after my little brother, David, was born. The village's only physician, Dr. Blackstone, had been out of town. By the time the ambulance drove my mother 40 miles to the hospital in Cleveland, she had slipped into a coma. A precious woman named Elizabeth Jones came to care for my brother and me during the long months while Mom was recuperating.

Lizzie, as we affectionately called her, wasn't a relative. She was a rotund black woman who had a heart as large as the girth that surrounded it. My family couldn't have afforded to pay her much of a salary, but even as a little girl I sensed that this compassionate caretaker would make everything all right.

My mother regained consciousness after a few months, but she was never able to regain her strength completely. After Mom was released from the Cleveland Clinic, Lizzie stayed on to care for us. We grew up being loved by our parents and by a saintly woman whose skin was the color of rich mahogany. You would have thought my mother was the baby sister that Lizzie never had, because she looked after her with such a watchful eye.

This all happened during the racially turbulent sixties, but I didn't know anything about racism. Not yet a first grader, I couldn't imagine anyone hating such a wonderful woman simply for the color of her skin. From the time I was a little girl, Lizzie was an example of colorblind love, because she cared for David and me as if we were her own children. I will forever cherish the memory of Lizzie's massive arms hugging me to her bountiful chest.

One of the ways Lizzie showed her love was through her Southern home cooking. If it hadn't been for my rapid metabolism, I probably would have ended up being as big as she was. I know Daddy had to have his pants let out more than once. Miss Lizzie is also the one responsible for my culinary talents. She patiently taught me how to bake all the pies and cakes that eventually won me countless blue ribbons at our county fair. She showed me how to make the best barbeque ribs and chicken anyone ever tasted this side of the Mississippi, too.

It was Lizzie who helped me make the right choice when it came to my husband. Since my mother battled health issues that left her with little energy, and my father worked long hours as the village solicitor, Lizzie was the one who became my faithful confidant.

It started when I was a little girl. Lizzie would tuck me in bed at night, pulling the soft covers up to my chin, and tell me a story. She would sit on the chair next to my bed wrap her calloused big hand around my tiny hand, and say, "Baby, I'm going to tell you a story about a princess." Whatever fairytale Lizzie told me, at the end she would always be sure to say, "And they lived happily ever after." Then, if I hadn't fallen asleep already, she would look at me intensely with her deep brown eyes and add, "And that's what you are going to do, child. You are going to find the man of your dreams, because every night I pray that God will have a special prince for my little Katie."

Lizzie wanted me to be happy, because she adored her husband, James Jones, who was the first black deputy in the county. After taking care of our family all day, she would rush to get home to him. Tragically, their only child, Jimmy Jr., was killed in a construction accident while he was working in Alabama. When I was in sixth grade, I heard Lizzie sobbing something awful one afternoon when I came home from school. My mama was holding her real tight, and she just kept repeating over and over in a soft voice, "It's going to be all right, Elizabeth. It's going to be all right."

My mother's attempt to soothe Lizzie only made her sob louder. "Oh, Lord, not my child! Not my Jimmy. Please, God, not my baby!" she shrieked while tightly clutching the phone's receiver in her hand. My mother couldn't pry the phone from her. Lizzie later said that she was terrified that if she hung it up, the dreadful news she had just received would become real. Mother patiently held her and patted her ample back as though she were a colicky infant. I stood in the doorway, feeling helpless and frightened, because I was used to Lizzie being the one to take care of all of us.

My second mother was a lot quieter after her son died, and her eyes lost their joyful sparkle. Then two events seemed to bring her back to life. First, a couple months after Jimmy's death, she learned that his young wife, Melba, was carrying their first child. Melba was staying in Alabama with her folks and hadn't told anyone about the pregnancy until she was six months along. When Jimmy was killed, the shock had almost caused her to miscarry.

When Lizzie found out she was going to be a grandmother, she started to come to life again, knitting both blue and pink blankets and two tiny sweaters for a boy or girl, explaining you had to be prepared. Three months later, Jimmy's wife delivered a healthy baby girl, Jasmine Elizabeth Jones, who weighed almost 8 pounds.

When the first photographs of Jasmine arrived, this time she sobbed with joy, saying, "Look at the beautiful smile. She has her daddy's smile." After that, whenever a new photo came, the proud grandma would grin from ear to ear. Jasmine visited her grandparents frequently, and eventually moved near here to attend Kent State University. Today, she's a psychologist specializing in family therapy on the staff at the Cleveland Clinic.

Anyway, the second event that brought healing to Lizzie's broken heart happened some years later on the night when I brought Jacob Montague home for dinner. We were high-school sweethearts, although Jake was a couple of years ahead of me. I'd met him when he was just beginning his senior year at Maple Grove High School. I'd been a self-conscious, 15-year-old sophomore attending my first homecoming dance with a couple of girlfriends. My parents wouldn't allow me to date until I was 16, so I had turned down Bobby Elliott's invitation to go to the dance with him.

Bobby was also a sophomore. He was popular with almost everyone because his family had a lot of money. His constant bragging and over-inflated view of himself didn't impress me much. Maybe because Bobby was short in stature, he over-compensated by being loud-mouthed.

I was relieved that I had a good excuse not to date Bobby, especially since I had heard that he had a way of getting girls alone in a vacant classroom at dances. I wasn't ready to deal with that yet. I had been a tomboy all my life, and I was afraid that if Bobby tried his tricks on me, I might sock him a good one.

My parents wouldn't let me date, but they thought it was fine that I attend the dance with my girlfriends, Patty and Donna. We were the inseparable three Musketeers who had been a trio since kindergarten.

I was so excited about my first dance that I spent an entire month sewing a short purple velvet jumper to wear. Mom and Lizzie took me shopping, and we bought a multi-patterned silk blouse with purple flowers that matched perfectly. It's embarrassing now, but I wore white go-go boots with purple fishnet hose to complete my outfit, since they were all the rage in the late sixties.

I was alone at the refreshment table at the dance, awkwardly eating a couple of store-bought cookies just for something to do, when Jacob Montague walked up, addressed me by my name, and asked me to dance.

"Katie, since you are the prettiest girl here, would you like to dance?" I almost spat the tasteless shortbread biscuit out. I was shocked not only that Jake had asked me to dance, but also that he knew who I was and thought I was pretty. Of course, I knew who he was. Every time I passed this handsome senior in the hallway at school, my heart would skip a beat.

Since I didn't answer right away, Jake thought I wasn't interested in dancing with him. He said, "I'm sorry, Katie, I guess you don't know me. My name is Jake Montague, I'm a senior. I hope that I wasn't too forward in asking you to dance."

He was older than me and had grown up on a farm outside of Maple Grove. We weren't ever formerly introduced, but I had had my eye on him for a few years. I washed down my cookie with some punch, and managed to reply, "Of course. I would love to dance with you, Jake."

What I was really thinking was, *Don't blow this, Katie girl. Be cool. Act nonchalant.* I was following my own advice, until Jake reached for my right hand with his left hand and intertwined his fingers with mine. Then he put his right hand on the small of my back and drew me to him as we began to dance. I knew at that moment that somehow I belonged with this tall handsome farm boy. Our destinies were connected, and there was no point in fighting the inevitable.

It wasn't so much the physical sensation of Jake holding me. Rather, it was the feeling of finding my place in the world, and my place was with him. That was our first dance, and a couple months later, under the mistletoe in a deserted hallway at a Christmas party at Patty's house, Jake and I shared our first kiss. That kiss sealed my fate, as all my tough tomboy resolve melted away when Jake's lips pressed against mine.

I was 16 then, and Jake and I were legally dating. I think my parents realized right away that Jake wasn't going to be a passing fancy, as they used to say. My late mother and father were honest, honorable people who asked only one thing of me. They asked me to promise that I would not give myself away to Jake or any man until my father had given me away as a bride.

It wasn't easy, because Jake and I had such a fiery passion for each other. But, because of my promise, Jake and I agreed that whatever it took, we would wait for our wedding day before we shared real intimacy.

"He's the one, baby. Jake's the prince I prayed for. I can see it when I look at you two together. You'll have to slow yourself down, child," Lizzie exclaimed that first night Jake had come for supper. After that, the sparkle returned to her eyes. She was busting with excitement, because she knew that somehow her prayers for me had been answered. God had supplied the prince she had wanted me to have.

The way Jake and I loved each other seemed bigger than the both of us sometimes. One night after supper, my dad cornered Jake in the living room while I was helping Lizzie with the dishes. Mother didn't do dishes, since she would be exhausted by early evening. Instead, she would lie down in her room and read her worn leather Bible, tattered from so much handling.

"Jacob, I want to ask you a favor," my father said matter-of-factly.

"Of course, Mr. Calloway. What can I do for you?"

"You can keep my daughter pure until you marry her." Jake laughed later, telling me that he nearly spat out the iced tea that he had just taken a gulp of right before my father made this request. "Young man, I wasn't born yesterday. I looked at my Agnes the same way you look at our Katherine.

I know you love her, and I would be honored to have you as a son-in-law one day." Jake said that Dad's voice got very firm and almost threatening when he added, "But for now, Jacob, I'll be expecting no less than your best."

"Yes, sir. I give you my promise to respect your daughter." My father didn't bring the subject up again, trusting that Jake's promise was sincere. Jake was more than sincere. He would have done anything for me, and I would have done anything for him. Maybe that's why, after we married, even though I was sad that Jake and I couldn't have children, it didn't devastate me. Instead we clung to each other, understanding that we were all we had.

Back in those days, women didn't have many career choices. You could either become a secretary, nurse, or a teacher. Since I didn't want to do any of those things, I learned how to help Jake around the farm and fix him and our few farm hands piping-hot meals every morning and night.

The years we spent together were wonderful, and they seemed to fly. Then after over four decades of waking up next to the love of my life, I found out my treasure of a husband had pancreatic cancer. He tried to fight it to stay with me. His gorgeous silver hair fell out from the chemotherapy, and his once athletic body became so thin I barely recognized him. When his doctor told me there wasn't any hope for recovery, at first I didn't know how I could go on without Jake in the world.

A few months later, right before he slipped into a coma and never regained consciousness, Jake reached for my hand.

Barely able to speak at that point, he labored to whisper, "Katie, you have been the best wife that any man could ever have. God knew that you were the woman I needed. You have to promise me you won't stop living when I'm gone." Jake coughed, and the rattle in his chest told me he would be leaving me really soon. "I'll see you again someday in Heaven. For now, though, the good Lord still has plans for you down here on this Earth." He held my hand as tight as he could and murmured the promise we had repeated to each other every single night for over forty years: "You are the love of my life, Katie Montague."

"You are the love of my life, Jake Montague." I could barely respond, choking back tears that wouldn't stop falling, I gently kissed his lips one final time. Then Jake closed his eyes for good. A couple hours later, he was gone.

I was lost the first year after Jake died. My conscientious spouse had left me well-off financially, but I didn't have a purpose any longer. My world seemed dull and meaningless without him in it.

Then, one night, I had a dream that I owned a coffee shop. In my dream, there were people seated at tables, laughing, drinking mugs of steaming coffee, and eating the prize-winning pies that I was famous for. My homemade cookies, fudge, and iced cinnamon rolls filled the glass display cases in the coffeehouse, too. Even though it was only a dream, I could smell the aroma of brewing coffee and almost taste the hot chocolate chip cookies I saw myself taking out of the oven. There I stood, in front of all these bottles of syrup that were used to make specialty coffee drinks, wearing an apron that was inscribed with "Katie's Coffee Corner" across the front.

The day before I dreamed about opening the coffee shop, I had said a simple prayer asking—more in desperation than faith—for something to hang onto. After all, I couldn't hold onto my Jake anymore; all I had were my memories of how inseparable we had been.

Being an old farmer's wife, I'm not one for supernatural signs. I'm a down-to-earth, practical woman who doesn't put much stock in spiritual phenomena. But, I have to tell you, that dream was so real that I started to think it might be my answer.

A couple of weeks later, while walking down Main Street, I saw the vacant, old brick house with a red and white "For Sale by Owner" sign in the front window. I had passed that house almost every day for the past year on my way to pick up the mail from my post office box. This was a task Jake had enjoyed doing before he died, because he got a kick out of teasing "Rita Rules," the postmistress.

Forty-eight-year-old Rita is attractive, even though she doesn't try to be. She is short and pleasantly plump. Her postal uniform is clean and starched, although she doesn't wear any makeup or jewelry. The Maple Grove native always pulls her shoulder-length, red hair back into a neat ponytail. Despite her lack of adornment, she is still pretty in an aging-country girl sort of way.

There has been some speculation about why she has never been a bride. Some say when Rita was in school, she fell in love with a boy from the Akron area. Things were different in that era, and he dumped her like a hot potato when his parents found out that her mother hadn't ever been married. Nobody knew who Rita's father was, but a few village old-timers said she looks a lot like a con man who passed through Maple Grove almost five decades ago selling water softeners that never arrived. Honestly, I think my old softie of a husband felt sorry for Rita, who is rapidly turning into an old maid.

Despite this, Rita is all business. She worked hard to get where she is, and like her or not, when the village's postmistress is around, the job always gets done. That's why folks voted for her to serve on the church board for the past three terms, even though a woman hadn't been on the board before. Last election, Maple Grove's library director, Sally Lewis, was nominated for a seat, and now the former school librarian is also a faithful board member.

As for Rita, she might not be real friendly, but everyone in Maple Grove trusts her. Jake used to say Rita was a good woman, and that's why he liked teasing her. "Oops, looks like I put the wrong postage on this letter," he would say jokingly. Or "Sorry, I forgot to add the zip code. Could you be a darling and look it up for me, Rita?"

"Please, do not address me as 'darling'!" she would almost shout shrilly. "My name is Rita, thank you very much."

Jake would laugh out loud when she would get frustrated with his antics and correct him or mutter something inaudible under her breath. He just enjoyed tormenting the poor woman. Because of this relationship, I was shocked when Rita cried inconsolably at Jake's funeral.

"I guess I enjoyed his teasing, just as much as he liked dishing it out," she told me at the funeral lunch the ladies of Maple Avenue Community Church had prepared. Rita was unceremoniously chewing a creamed chicken sandwich when she asked, "Did Jake ever tell you about the time last year that Mel Sanders came into the post office drunk and high, threatening to punch his wife Jolene who was in line buying some stamps? He wanted her to give him her money, and she refused."

It was a strange topic of conversation for a funeral luncheon, but I shook my head no, more out of politeness than interest.

"Jake stepped in between Mel and Jolene and firmly escorted Mel outside, warning him that if he hit Jolene, he would have to go through him to do it."

Now, this was interesting. "Oh, my goodness!" I started laughing uncontrollably, and everyone there began staring at me with concern, thinking that I was hysterical with grief. Jake probably didn't tell me this tale, because he might have thought I would call him an "old fool" for standing up to Mel.

He knew it would have frightened me, because Mel Sanders is almost 30 years younger than Jacob was, and in lot better shape. Mel had been a high school wrestling champion, but injuries his freshman year of college cut off his scholarship money and made him bitter.

The past fifteen years of too many beers and abusing pain

medication were beginning to take a visible toll on the once athletic man. Jolene, Mel's wife and high school sweetheart, had stuck with him through thick and thin. Even after he became physically abusive, she refused to leave him, even though lots of people tried to help her. When he became violent, she would stay at the Maple Grove Inn for a couple days, until he calmed down. A previous pastor had addressed Mel's addiction problem once, but all he got for his effort was a black eye. People were pretty sure that Mel was using heroin now, too.

Hearing this story about my Jake protecting Jolene made me proud. Eventually, I stopped laughing and instantly started sobbing for the wonderful husband I had just buried. For a moment, Rita reached out and hugged me so tightly that I could barely breathe. Then she let me go and straightened the collar of her blouse as if she were somehow trying to put her life back in order. I had no idea how I was going to find any order in my own shattered existence, but gradually I did. After Jake's death, I started picking up the mail each morning. I looked forward to seeing Rita. Every day, I passed the empty brick house that would become my coffee shop, but I didn't notice the "For Sale" sign until a couple weeks after my "coffee shop" dream.

Some years back, the Victorian structure had served as both the office and residence of Maple Grove's only family physician. Now, there was a brand-new clinic just outside the village, staffed by doctors from the Cleveland area.

The late Dr. Macklin Blackstone, affectionately called

"Doc" by all of us whom he took care of for almost six decades, had practiced medicine until he was well into his eighties. He died just a few months short of his 89th birthday. There hadn't been a Mrs. Blackstone, since Doc had been too busy tending to other people's families to have one of his own.

The Blackstone place sat vacant for a couple of years, because no one really knew what to do with it. The old building would need a lot of work to renovate it. But, all of the sudden, when I saw that "For Sale" sign in the window, a plan formulated in my mind. I would sell the farm, move into Doc's apartment in the house, and turn the office area into a coffee shop.

Selling my small farm wouldn't be any problem. Ever since Jake passed away, "old" Ed Hardy, my closest neighbor and the most successful farmer in our county, had been hounding me to let him buy it. I hadn't wanted to let the farm go, because it was all I had left of Jake.

For the first time since my husband's death, I felt hope rise up inside of me. Instantly, I began to mentally set the wheels in motion to open Katie's Coffee Corner. Little did I know that a year after I started my business venture, Cassandra Martin would walk into my shop and become like a daughter to me.

Chapter 3
Getting to Know Each Other

CASSIE DIDN'T TALK much at first when she visited my little cafe. Usually, she would bring a book in and read as she drank her coffee. Once in a while, she would be dressed up especially pretty and be more talkative than normal. It seemed it was on these days that she would order a sugar-free caramel latte without whipped cream instead of a cup of the flavor of the day.

"Could you please make my latte really hot?" she would say each time she ordered the specialty coffee. Soon, I learned to make them just the way she liked. Then, before she could get the words out, I would tease, "Really hot, right?" Cassie would smile, happy that someone knew what she liked, but I had a funny feeling that no one, not even her husband, really knew her. There was something strangely mysterious about the new pastor's wife.

"When I was young, living in Philadelphia and working at the museum, I would treat myself to a latte every Friday to celebrate getting through another work week," she once told me. Before long, I observed it was usually every Tuesday late afternoon, not Friday, when Cassie ordered her latte now. Other days, it was a flavored coffee in a ceramic mug.

Why was I drawn to this 41-year-old stranger? We were over two decades apart in chronological age, and there was something lonesome about Cassie triggering my maternal instincts. I quickly perceived she was such an incredible actress that I was virtually the only one who seemed to notice how very lonely she was.

In my coffee shop or Sunday after church, I would watch Cassie listen intently to people as they shared their problems with her. She was compassionate and sympathetic to their needs, always suggesting a solution, promising to pray, or offering a hug.

After I got to know her, I once asked, "Does it bother you when people tell you their personal problems, assuming it's your job to listen because you are the pastor's wife?"

"No. It energizes me in a strange sort of way. Even though John is the pastor, it really is like God gave me a ministry to listen." She took a sip of her highlander grog, a flavor of the day. "I know often they are talking to me because they want me to relay the information to my husband, since he is their minister, but that really is okay with me."

Then she smiled an impish grin. "I don't always pass information on. If it's important, I tell him right away, but if it's something insignificant, like two women fighting over what kind of flowers to put on the altar, I don't bother John with it." She chuckled; everybody knew that Evelyn Schroeder and Mattie Burkholder were constantly fighting over flowers. It was all harmless, as they were eighty-something widows with lots of money and more time on their hands than they knew what to do with. It actually seemed they enjoyed their ongoing feud.

Funny thing is, nobody at the contemporary service even knows about the altar flowers. The younger crowd likes to dim the sanctuary chandeliers and then place about a dozen candles in large colored-glass globes scattered all over the platform.

Cassie doesn't worry about flowers or candles. She just seems to love everyone, despite their flaws.

"To a lot of folks, I'm anonymous," she said. "I can't tell you how much I hated this when I first married John."

"What do you mean, 'anonymous'?" I asked. "Everyone wants to know the pastor's wife."

She chuckled again, this time a bit resignedly. "You would think that, but the truth is that often when people speak with John, even if I'm standing right next to him, they don't ask my name or include me in their conversation." She saw the look of shock on my face. "Katie, they don't even glance at me, especially not when they first meet us." I shook my head in disbelief.

"In the beginning of our marriage, John didn't notice how people would overlook my presence. After all, when congregants have a chance to speak with their preacher, they usually have a lot on their minds. It's a pastor's job to listen to their troubles, so I tried not to fault them for not including me, but I did feel like an outsider."

"How did you work this out?" I didn't want to pry into Cassie's business, but she needed someone to talk to. "It seems everyone at the church really gravitates to you now."

"John started consciously including me in conversations by asking my opinion, or just by physically pulling me to his side. He would say, 'I know you want to speak with my wife, Cassie, too. She really is my better half, and we're a team.'" Suddenly, the brunette minister's wife grew very serious. "Katie, you know, what's difficult is when I can tell that John is carrying a really heavy burden, and he can't share it with me."

This confused me, as Jake and I had shared everything. Besides, I didn't know what a heavy burden was. "Not sure I've heard the term 'heavy burden.' What does that mean, Cassie girl?" I began brewing a fresh pot of snickerdoodle decaf, and turned my cell phone ringer off.

"Oh, I guess that's church talk for when someone is extremely concerned about something. For example, I can almost visibly see my husband emotionally weighted down with concern when a parishioner tells him something that he can't share, due to ministerial confidentiality."

Cassie took a bite of a banana nut bread muffin I had just baked that morning and chewed thoughtfully for a moment. "Did you ever think about the fact that a pastor is often the first one to find out someone in the congregation has cancer, or maybe that they are having an affair, or that they have a child who's gotten into trouble?"

"Not really," I admitted honestly.

"I can tell it breaks his heart when the hearts of the people he pastors are broken, and he can't even tell me what's wrong. He is a man of integrity when it comes to keeping a confidence. Of course, most often, everyone in the church eventually finds out, but frequently John carries a secret for a long time before the rest of us know."

"I never thought of that. After Jake died, I did wonder what it's like for a minister to be the one to comfort the family when there's been a death. I don't remember too much about the first few months, because I was grieving so severely that it all seems like such a blur."

Our former pastor, Michael Johnson, was there for both of us when Jake had pancreatic cancer. Pastor Mike and his wife, Barb, barely left my side in the days following Jake's death.

He retired from the church a decade earlier, but we remained close friends. Besides, Maple Avenue Community Church went through several new ministers in the years after Mike's retirement. We didn't have time to bond with any of them before they moved on. Two had better opportunities they said, but one pastor resigned after he got into a heated argument with board member Ed Hardy Sr., who doesn't care much for change of any kind. Everyone believed the argument started when the young minister who had studied church growth wanted to take out the pews and replace them with padded chairs to accommodate more people, but no one knew for sure.

On the other hand, Mike was M.A.C.'s senior pastor for over twenty years. After his retirement, the couple relocated to Florida. I couldn't believe they came back to be with us during those last couple weeks of Jake's illness; although it shouldn't have surprised me, because Mike loved Jake like a brother.

I could tell it wasn't easy for him to preach my husband's funeral message. When they went back to Florida, I'd felt lost. Then, Pastor John Martin had shown up with his beautiful wife. I looked at Cassie intently, feeling blessed to have her in my life. I said a silent prayer that the Martins wouldn't be passing through like their three predecessors had. Despite the upheaval, the church didn't decline in attendance during all the transition. I think people attended on Sunday curious to see what would happen next, because in a little village like Maple Grove there isn't too much excitement.

Speaking of excitement, my coffee shop door opened, and in walked Jolene Sanders. *Her eye must be black again,* I suspected, *because she has dark glasses on, and it's an overcast morning.* At that moment, I was proud of Cassie, who quickly cut our conversation short and said, "Katie, I would like to buy Jolene a cup of coffee."

Jolene slid into a remote booth. Cassie followed her and sat down beside her. Next thing, I saw Cassie put her arm around Jolene, who began to sob. I had heard that Jolene had warmed up to Cassie, but I was amazed. Cassie had never mentioned her relationship with Jolene to me, despite all of our chats.

Like her husband, Cassie didn't share the confidences of the individuals to whom she ministered.

I took a cup of coffee to the table and set it in front of Jolene. I couldn't help but overhear Cassie say, "Jolene, God does not want you to live this way. He doesn't want anyone to hurt you. You are His child."

I had to walk away quickly, because I didn't want to invade their privacy, even though I was fuming with indignation. *For goodness' sake, Jolene, don't let this man keep hitting you. Cassie's right: God doesn't want you to live this way, and neither do any of us here in Maple Grove who have known you since you were a little girl.* But I kept my thoughts to myself, since my minister's spouse seemed to have the situation under control.

Besides becoming a spiritual daughter, Cassie was becoming a close friend. I not only loved her, but I respected her, because of the heart she had for others like Jolene. But, isn't that what mothers and daughters do, become friends when their daughters grow up?

It wasn't as if Cassie needed a mother. Her own mother, Diana Kirk, was very much alive and part of her daughter's life. Or, as much a part of her life as she could be, living in Philadelphia. But there were secrets locked inside Cassie that not even her mother knew about. For some reason, Cassie eventually chose to tell me her tragic tale a little at a time.

Cassie would share a bit of her past history each time she stopped in my shop, if there weren't any other customers around. Some days, it seemed almost providential how the coffeehouse remained void of patrons when she popped in. After she left, the tables would fill up once again. It was as though someone much more powerful than either of us wanted her to get her story out, so that she could finally heal.

Don't get me wrong, Cassie is also a wonderful listener. She wanted to hear all about my life with Jake. For my part, Cassie gave me a new purpose, just like the coffee shop had, because she made me feel needed again.

One day I told her, "Jake was such a big tough brute of a man, but like most husbands, he craved my support." I took a picture of Jake and me on our wedding day off the counter next to the cash register and handed it to Cassie. "We married right after my high school graduation because of our promise to my parents that we would wait for our wedding night to be together. The chemistry between us fueled by our youthful love couldn't be denied."

Cassie blushed, but she nodded for me to tell her more. "To put the fire out, we said our vows on a gorgeous June day in the sanctuary of Maple Avenue Community Church. Then we had a beautiful picnic reception on the front lawn of Jake's family farm. That farm became ours after Jake's brother decided to become a veterinarian and his father died in the early eighties."

I absentmindedly wiped the wooden countertop that separated Cassie and me with a wet towel. "In the beginning of our marriage, I didn't understand how much my words and actions affected Jake. We married so young that our immaturity caused us both to be stubborn and selfish. When

I got angry, I would sulk and stop talking to him for days. Even worse, once I left and went to Cleveland and stayed with a girlfriend."

"You left Jake?" The pastor's wife seemed shocked.

"Yes, but let me tell you the whole story first. It was Lizzie who called to try to get me to come back home. Her words still echo in my mind. 'Child, what do you think you are doing, leaving your young husband like this?'

"'He treats me like I don't even matter to him, Lizzie,' I answered sobbing, 'His mother can be so picky. She insults me about everything, from my housekeeping to the kind of clothes I wear.' I was trying my best to defend my actions.

"'Jake told me his mama's been giving you a bit of a hard time, baby.' *A bit of a hard time...was that ever an understatement.* 'He's real sorry about that, but he's not quite sure how to fix it. You see, it's his mama, and she doesn't mean anything by it. Let me tell you a little secret: a lot of mothers-in-law are like that, even though they don't mean to be,' said the woman who had always been like a second mother to me.

"'It's just that Mrs. Montague loves her boy so much. Two women should never live in the same house together, at least not when they love the same man, even if it is in different ways. I know it's been hard on you, staying with his folks since you married. Jake understands that you need a place of your own, and he's trying to figure out how he can afford to do that.'

"There was a long pause, and then Lizzie warned, 'Jake

has dark circles under his eyes, and I swear he's lost 10 pounds since you've been gone.' Jake was already too thin, and he always got sick when he didn't get his rest. I held the phone receiver tightly to my ear and listened more intently as Lizzie's lecture continued.

"'Don't you know that boy is lost without you, baby? Men can't tell you they need you when they are young. Someday, when you're both old, he'll tell you. For now, he's trying to act strong and tough, but inside of every man there's this little boy who needs the woman he loves to stay by his side.'

"Lizzie's call really got to me. I kept thinking about what she said, then I got into my old black VW bug and headed back to the farm. By the following spring, Jake and I had bought a used house trailer on payments. We set up housekeeping on the Montague place, about a mile from the main homestead where Jake's parents lived. It was like our little palace. A few years later, we built a home of our own there.

"Lizzie didn't shame me by ever bringing the incident up, but I'm glad I followed her wise advice and stopped all that nonsense of fighting my husband over every unimportant decision. I began to understand what Lizzie meant when she warned that a man is like a little boy inside when it comes to the woman he loves.

"After I figured all this out, by faith every night when my husband and I would lie down in bed I would whisper in his ear, 'You are the love of my life, Jake Montague,' right before he would go to sleep. Even if I was upset with Jake for something, I still understood that little boy inside of him needed to know I loved him, despite our differences.

"Before too long, he started whispering it back to me: 'You are the love of my life, Katie Montague.' He also began trusting me when he needed someone to talk to. My steadfast love made him feel safe enough to show his vulnerable side. When a problem with the farm would arise, we would talk it out. Although I had little advice to give about farming, Jake said my listening enabled him to put his situation in perspective."

When I finished my story, Cassie was beginning to cry. "You were supposed to tell me this today, Katie. John rarely talks to me about any of his concerns, or even his goals. I had no idea there was a little boy inside of a grown man."

Tears were streaming down her beautiful cheeks. She was crying harder now, and I didn't understand what had made her cry. She didn't know me well enough to trust me with her secrets yet. Even though we had been having our talks for almost a year, it wasn't time.

Chapter 4
A Family's Secret

THE JOB OF listening to Cassie became a labor of love for me. I didn't ever tire of hearing my surrogate daughter pour her heart out, as she somehow had worked her way into mine. Whenever she would stop at Katie's Coffee Corner, she told me personal things from long ago that had changed her forever.

At first, Cassie relayed her harmless high school history. Once she showed me a photo of her with her parents taken only weeks before her dad's death. "When you were a teenager you had the same long brown hair and naturally thick lashes that highlight your captivating hazel eyes," I said studying the picture that she held. "I'll bet your girlfriends teased you about your 'cover girl' figure, even though they probably couldn't help but envy how your male classmates must have competed for your attention. You look so much like your beautiful mother, except for her blonde hair." I smiled and set a very hot latte in front of my minister's spouse.

Cassie glanced around self-consciously even though the

cafe was momentarily deserted following the lunch rush. She was embarrassed by my description of her and what she was about to tell. "I guess you could say I was a hit with the boys." She blew on the steaming concoction I had whipped up for her, and took a cautious sip. "For some reason, it was always the 'bad boys' who pursued me, the ones whose intentions were less than honorable. Of course, John wasn't like that. In high school I was a 'good girl,' but this was more a result of my fear of letting anyone get close than an obedience to following all the rules I had been taught in Sunday school."

I nodded, afraid that if I spoke she might stop talking.

"Don't get me wrong: due to my naïve ways I was hurt rather badly during my senior year, when I trusted a boy who proved to be untrustworthy. I was an impressionable cheerleader, and our school's football captain, Tim Drake, was determined that I would be his trophy girlfriend."

Cassie seemed far away, as if she were traveling back in time. "Tim even ran off the field during our homecoming game senior year at Lancaster High to give me a dozen red roses that one of the water boys smuggled in for him. That got Tim in a lot of trouble, but not before I fell for his All-American charm and good looks."

She looked down at her wedding ring, then back up at me. "Nothing happened, Katie. I was a church girl raised with good morals, and I refused to let Tim get past first base in the backseat of his souped-up Firebird. When football season ended, so did our romance."

It was odd, because instead of sadness, Cassie's face

flushed a bright red and her voice sounded agitated. So I asked, "Are you still angry at him for some reason?"

"It hurt me when Tim dumped me to take out a leggy sophomore named Tammy Bart. But, it hurt me even more why he did it. Tammy had short, bleached blonde hair and wore way too much makeup. By the time she was in middle school, rumor was that Tammy's stepfather had forced his way to a lot more than first base with her."

Outrage showed in Cassie's eyes. "Then, in eighth grade, Tammy began dressing suggestively and stopped caring about her schoolwork. That's when the jocks started passing her around, but nobody claimed Tammy as a girlfriend."

Because of her tender heart, Cassie felt sorry for Tammy. It really disgusted her that Tim was like the other guys who used the poor girl. "Nobody spoke too much about sexual abuse back then, Katie. Her stepfather would be charged with a crime, if that happened today. I was furious when Tim had the nerve to call me to apologize for taking Tammy out. The way I saw it, he was probably done using her. Tammy's checkered reputation prevented a boy like Tim from taking her to the prom, and he needed a date."

"What happened to Tammy is very disturbing, and Tim's ego is unbelievable. Cassie, how could he have possibly considered you'd be willing to be his girlfriend again?"

"I guess he did, because he asked rather casually if I could forgive him. Sounding downright charitable, he offered to escort me to prom reassuring me he would be glad to take me, if I didn't have a date."

42

I shook my head in disgust at this boy's actions.

"Katie, I was so angry I didn't answer. I slammed the phone down hard and never talked to Tim again." Her heart hadn't been broken, but Cassie had been bruised pretty badly by this encounter.

Even as a teenager, she figured out Tammy Bart was not the type of girl a football captain took out in public. Cassie certainly wasn't going to be the one to stand beside a cold-hearted jock like Tim, who could care less about using a lost young girl for his own pleasure. Part of the reason Cassie had the courage to do this was because of the advice her father had given her. Even though her dad died a week before Cassie's 14th birthday, she vividly recalled him emphasizing over and over, "Don't settle for anything less than the best. You're Daddy's princess, so wait until your prince comes along."

Her father's wise words echoed the same message I had heard from my second mother years before. Cassie couldn't help but realize right away that Tim Drake was no prince. All he ever tried to do was to push her into doing something she knew she would regret. She was grateful that for some reason her father had been unrelenting when it came to this message of waiting for the best.

It wasn't that same day but another late Tuesday afternoon not too long after when Cassie told me about the circumstances surrounding her dad's death. Then I began to partially understand why her eyes had that haunted look. Sadly, Benjamin Kirk had left Cassie and her mother, Diana, only questions when he took his own life one tragic night. "He didn't even leave a note for us, Katie, like many folks who commit suicide do." Cassie's voice was racked with confusion while tears filled her eyes.

The cafe had just closed for the day, but I set a mug of fresh caramel cream decaf in front of her, and handed her a tissue. I didn't think caffeine would be a good idea, because she was already visibly shaken by her memories. "I'm so sorry, sweetie. I hope you will be able to tell me what happened," I urged patting her hand.

I had prepared myself a late lunch of homemade ham-and-bean soup and cornbread. Cassie said she wasn't hungry, because she had eaten earlier. I sat down next to her at the counter, but before I began eating, I prayed aloud, "Dear God, thank you for my food, and please give my precious friend the courage to face the truth about her father. Give me the wisdom to know how to be your listening ear in Jesus' name. Amen." Then while buttering my cornbread, I said, "Why don't you start at the beginning, Cassie?"

"If you really want to hear it, Katie."

"Of course, I do. What was your father like?"

"Dad was a quiet and gentle man who'd kept things to himself. There was a twinkle in his eye and a perpetual crooked grin that seemed to say, 'I know something funny, but I'm not about to share it.'" Pulling open the tab of an individual creamer, she added the thick, white half and half to her coffee.

"My mother told me that it was my father's boyish good

looks, fun-loving attitude, and his belief that anything was possible that drew her to him when they met while serving in the Army in the late sixties during the Vietnam War. Mom was a nurse stationed stateside, and Dad was a 22-year-old private who had been drafted. They fell in love while he was in basic training in California. She was working in a military hospital there.

"They talked about getting married. Dad even bought her a diamond cluster ring shaped like a heart as a promise that they would someday be together. Mom still keeps that ring in her jewelry box. But, with a tour of active duty in the war zone looming on the horizon, my father decided against a rushed wedding, fearing he might leave her a grieving widow. When he was shipped overseas, Mom said she found herself 'praying every night that God would return him safely to her.' I guess other men probably asked her out, especially those in uniform, but the only man in uniform she was eager to see was her Ben."

"Well, since you look a lot like your mother did in that old photo, I'll bet she had to fight off the lonely young soldiers who were hoping for an opportunity to have a date with her," I joked lightheartedly, encouraging my pastor's wife to continue sharing memories of her family.

Cassie blushed like she always did when I complimented her. Then she continued. "It was in 1968, after serving a one-year tour in Vietnam seeing active combat, that Dad finally made it home. He wasn't injured, at least not physically like many other Army veterans were.

"They married almost immediately, and for a few years Mom believed that Dad was happy. Then something went terribly wrong. It took my mother time to see that her beloved Ben was not the same. My father's unforgettable smile was gone, and so was his spontaneous laughter. Some mornings, he had to drag himself out of bed to get to his job at his family's dental lab.

"I shouldn't have read my mother's diary, but I found it on her dresser shortly after he died. I was a grieving teenage girl, desperate for answers. Mom wrote about hearing what sounded like my father crying in the shower occasionally, but the mournful wails were muffled, so she wasn't sure what she should do. When she asked Dad about it, he flatly denied it, although his eyes were sunken and ringed with red. Her exact words were, *'There was a darkness about him, a nearly visible cloud of depression tormenting him.'*

"In 1974, Mom recorded an entry about discovering she was pregnant with me, and how my father seemed to become more optimistic almost immediately. He worked every night in his workshop after being on his job all day, to make a hand-crafted crib of cherry wood.

"While he was working on it, he wouldn't let my mother see it. When she was eight months pregnant, Dad unveiled the beautiful crib that he had created, and she was amazed at both the finished product and by his exquisite workmanship. She had no idea that my father was capable of handcrafting such a beautiful piece of furniture."

"Your birth must have been such a blessing, such a gift of

restoration for your parents," I said having a fleeting moment of sadness never having experienced the birth of a child of my own.

"My mother's diary entry was so descriptive, '*When our daughter, Cassandra Marie Kirk, was born, Ben's spirits couldn't have been higher. He passed out cigars throughout the hospital, kissed me repeatedly, and insisted on taking countless pictures of our baby girl through the nursery glass. His hopeful attitude remained for over five years after we took Cassie home. My Ben loved being a dad, and everyone around him could visibly see his joy.*'

"Then for some reason, my mother realized that Dad's depression returned." Cassie swirled the now cold coffee around in the bottom of her mug. "At first, it confused me when my normally playful father began to sit in a chair and stare at the wall without talking. This would go on night after night, although during the day he seemed able to hold it together for his job. Mom felt helpless in knowing how to ease his suffering, because his distant behavior was causing her to suffer too.

"She begged in desperation for him to get some help, telling him, 'There's no shame in going to counseling.' Even as a little girl, I would overhear them arguing about this, especially after I started school. There were also the nightmares. Sometimes, my father would go to sleep, and later wake up drenched in sweat and screaming for help, but he refused to discuss these dreams. Mom guessed he thought he was back in the Vietnam jungles fighting for his life, or maybe taking the life of someone else."

I shook my head listening to the familiar account, realizing that Cassie's father was suffering from what we now identify as post-traumatic stress disorder, but little was known about this condition then. Ben Kirk's existence was a typical but tragic tale of a war veteran's life gradually spiraling out of control after returning stateside.

"When I started middle school, dad had a really difficult time getting to work some days, but he still went. After drinking most of the night, he would awaken from a fitful sleep with a splitting headache from a hangover.

"Finally, when I was 13, my father lost his job after punching a client who said he didn't think the U.S. should have ever been part of the Vietnam War. This was the last straw for my grandfather, who owned the dental lab. It wasn't just hitting the customer, although Dad was arrested for the assault. He had also been making costly mistakes at work and upsetting the personnel at the dental offices the lab supplied. 'It breaks my heart, but I have to fire you, Ben,' my granddad said handing him his last paycheck. 'I never thought it would come to this, but you're beginning to wreak havoc wherever you go. I kept you on for as long as I could because you're my son, but I can't risk your violent outbursts with our clients anymore.'"

"That must have been excruciating for your grandfather as well as your family. How did you survive financially?"

"My mother was working full-time as a registered nurse,

ensuring that our little family could pay the bills and have health benefits. Dad must have appreciated her carrying this load, but being the man, he thought of himself as the main breadwinner. That's why, when he got fired, his world really did fall apart.

"Mom always feared that losing his job would be rock bottom for him, and it was. After that, my father couldn't dig himself out of the downward spiral of chronic depression. He didn't even try to dress in the morning or take a shower, and would start drinking right away."

"You must have been so afraid that your father was going to do something to harm himself, Cassie? I can't imagine the terrible tension your household was under." I ate my last spoonful of ham and bean soup, and pushed the bowl away.

"I was too young to understand what was really happening. My mother told me she had no idea my father would hurt himself either. That one evening she would wake up at 3:45 a.m. after hearing what sounded like a bang and find Dad's side of the bed empty. But that wasn't unusual, because he often drank into the late hours of the night. As a first shift nurse, she typically slept soundly until 5:30 a.m., since she had to be at the hospital by 7:00.

"Eerily, that particular night when the loud pop awakened her, she had a sick feeling in the pit of her stomach. Mom searched the house quietly for Dad, not wanting to wake me, because I hadn't stirred at the disturbing sound. The fear she felt heightened with each empty room. She had nowhere left to search but the garage. Relief flooded her initially when she opened the garage door and saw my father's old truck sitting in its predictable spot.

"Then, horror gripped her, as she saw the body of a man slumped over the wheel. Instinctively, she put her hand to her mouth to muffle the scream that was rising from deep inside her. She could hear the blood-curdling wail as it was coming out, because her hand did little to stop it.

"Mom's shrill shriek awakened me from a deep sleep. Within seconds, I rushed to the garage to find out what had happened. Maybe because I was an only child or because Dad had been so ill for much of my life, I was very close with my mom when I was young. I knew her like I knew myself. Because of our intuitive familiarity, I'd sensed that my mother would only scream like that if someone had died.

"By the time I reached her side, she was frantically checking my dad's wrist for a pulse. When Mom saw me, she tried to regain control of herself to protect me. She told me to call 911, that my father had been shot. Being a trained nurse, my mother already knew that there was no need for the ambulance to hurry; my father had ended his mental torment with a single bullet just moments earlier." I overheard her tell all of this later to the police officer for a report.

"Unaware that my dad was dead, I ran to the phone and frantically dialed the 911 dispatcher, begging her to send help quickly. 'My father's been shot. No, there's not an intruder. Please, hurry. He's bleeding badly from a head wound.'

"I gave the dispatcher our address, and again, desperate

to save my father, I hysterically pleaded, 'Hurry!' Without answering any more of the dispatcher's questions, I set the phone down not hanging up and ran back to the garage, where I found my mother with tears streaming down her cheeks as she held the lifeless body of the man whom she had loved fervently despite his mental illness and addiction. It was then I realized my father was gone. He abandoned us whether he meant to or not, Katie."

"I understand you so much better now," I whispered sympathetically, not wanting to disrupt the mood. Despite only being a teenager, confronted with the desolation caused by unexpected agonizing grief, Cassie sensed that her life would never be the same. A part of her innocence died with her father. The world was no longer safe, and people were no longer trustworthy. The man who had brought her into the world and promised to take care of her, had taken his own life without so much as a thought of her. At least, that was the way she must have felt. "Are you able to finish the story today, Cassie? I know there's more."

"Katie, thanks for caring so much," she almost whimpered, while nervously smoothing her long hair. "I haven't gotten to the worst part yet. You see, an ambulance with two paramedics, a fire engine staffed with four firefighter/paramedics, and two police cruisers arrived at almost the exact same time. While the paramedics began working on my father, the law officers started asking questions, and suddenly I became aware that my mother and I were under some sort of suspicion regarding my father's death. Despite the paramedics' valiant efforts, it was also obvious they couldn't revive Dad.

"'Are you sure he shot himself? There wasn't any kind of altercation, was there?' A tough-looking, middle-aged patrolwoman directed the questions to my grief-stricken parent. Due to her medical background, Mom remained abnormally composed after her initial scream and torrent of tears grasping the finality of my father's action. Hearing the accusing tone during the officer's interrogation, shock gave way to rage, and her calm façade crumbled. 'What? Are you suggesting I shot the man who was my soul mate? The man who I promised to be with 'in sickness and in health'?'" Mom almost shouted back. Then she broke down. Her mournful wailing filled the small garage like a caged animal caught in a trap. I hugged her tightly while crying almost inaudibly myself. My mother was loud enough for the both of us.

"'Why, God? Why?' my mother moaned between her sobs. The female officer grew suddenly silent. Then an older paramedic/firefighter named Larry Wagner, who knew my mother professionally through her work as a nurse from his hospital runs, put his arm around her, and said, 'I know it seems insensitive, Diana, but the questions are just routine. The officer is only trying to do her job.' He lowered his voice almost to a whisper, 'So many times, we don't know why, but that doesn't mean that God doesn't care about what you are going through.' Mom regained her composure and stopped sobbing, frantically clutching onto Larry's words as if they were some sort of lifeline.

"'When I lost my wife to cancer, Diana, I asked God, 'Why?' over and over. After awhile, I realized there wasn't going to be an answer. But He was there to help me through it. He is going to be with you every step of the way now too.'

"I stood at my mother's side, not leaving her alone for a moment. Larry reached out and encircled both of us with his strong arms as the other paramedics gently lifted my father's body onto a stretcher. I buried my face in my mom's shoulder as the first responders loaded the gurney with the lifeless form into the back of the ambulance.

"It was then that I made a silent vow. *I will never let a man get close enough to me to abandon me ever again.* I kept this vow for years following my father's death."

It took a while, but Cassie was able to tell me the whole heartbreaking story. It became obvious why she struggled with abandonment issues, and why it was difficult for her to bond with people – even people she loved. After all, that is what she felt that her father had done: he'd abandoned her and her mother. He'd left them when he didn't have to. He left no note, no explanation, and no plan for how she and her mom would survive.

In the days that followed, her mother tried to explain to Cassie about the distressing dark moods that enveloped her father on occasion. How without warning, his disposition could turn from joy to desperation. Cassie didn't care about clinical terms like bipolar (better known back then as manic depression), mood swings, or post-traumatic stress disorder; she just wanted her father back.

"It's my fault," Cassie's grandfather sobbed when he heard the news. "I shouldn't have fired him. He might still be here, if only I hadn't let him go."

"Oh, I should have insisted he get help," wailed Ben's inconsolable mother. Like Diana, she thought, *If I had just loved him more. Loved him better, I could have somehow helped to ease his emotional pain.*

Even Cassie secretly blamed herself, confessing the reasons that had always made her feel guilty about the pressure she might have put on her dad. "Katie, I always wanted him to do so much for me. I was forever hounding him to get us a bigger house, and a horse. I wanted private art lessons, and clothes and shoes. I was never happy with all the things I had."

Maybe that was why Cassie couldn't tell her husband that she longed to have a home of her own. She was beyond tired of living in parsonages, but after her father's death, she refused to want material possessions too badly. She carried this untrue but deeply imbedded belief that her desire for things had pushed her father into feeling like a failure.

In reality, a part of Ben Kirk had died in the war, since he'd refused to get help or talk about his horrific memories. Other veterans had reached out to him when they'd seen him drowning his sorrows in alcohol, but he wouldn't listen or open up to anyone.

After his death, his heartbroken widow went through his dresser drawers to put his clothes in boxes for a local thrift store. It shocked her when she found countless bottles of prescription sleeping pills and tranquilizers hidden among her husband's belongings. He had been visiting a variety of physicians who were prescribing medications that he was overusing to make himself feel better.

Diana blamed herself for not seeing this. Cassie overheard her mother tell her father's parents why she felt she was the one responsible for her husband's suicide. "I'm a nurse. I should have realized that my husband was battling an addiction. Sometimes, when he was drunk, I would wonder how on earth a few beers or a couple of shots of whiskey could have such a dramatic impact. Now, I know it wasn't just the whiskey or beer. The pills were increasing the alcohol's effect. He was crying out for help, but I couldn't see it."

The truth is, nobody knew how bad it was. Ben hid his pain, and like most folks who struggle with mental health issues, his family didn't know how to intervene. He locked his emotional baggage so tightly inside himself that no one realized how tormented he really was. Ben even attended church regularly, and Diana suggested that he talk to their pastor about his depression. Ben refused to go, rationalizing that "A minister wouldn't understand the kind of things a man sees and has to do in war."

Cassie's father had been taught and erroneously believed that a strong man should find his own way, and so he didn't see any way out. His pride kept him from getting the help his broken spirit desperately needed, and his family began to believe that was why he killed himself. He'd started to feel he was a burden. When he was intoxicated, Cassie had heard her father mutter under his breath how they would be better off without him.

The more depressed he got, the more he drank. The more he drank, the more depressed he became. When Ben's family found out he had also been abusing medications, they figured he just got trapped in the vicious cycle that addiction produces.

I listened intently, not commenting during Cassie's account of her father's suicide and addiction battles, understanding it was a family secret she had concealed for decades. I was honored she had chosen to reveal it to me, and put my arm around her as she began to cry.

Wiping tears from my own eyes with a napkin, my heart was breaking for the unbearable loss and agonizing grief she had experienced. I thought, *Now, I understand why there is such a haunted look in Cassie's eyes.* It explained part of it— but not all of it, I would later discover.

"That's why I like coffee so much, Katie. Long ago, when I found out about my father's addiction, it destroyed any desire I had to experiment with alcohol or drugs fervently presuming they were responsible for taking my father from me. I was the one who found the empty whiskey bottle in the truck the night he shot himself."

Cassie avoided anything to do with alcohol after that. "The whole time I was dating the football captain, he tried to get me to drink. He would bring beer or wine along whenever we went out, but I didn't want any part of it. In my mind, all I could see was that liquor bottle lying next to my dad's body. The way Tim kept pushing me, it just gave me more resolve not to drink."

Saying, "No," to Tim and the other boys she dated was easy. During high school and in college, she went out with a couple of other young men, but nothing serious. Cassie simply kept her vow never to let anyone get close enough to abandon her. Her relationship with Tim convinced her that keeping her distance was a good thing, especially after he dumped her for Tammy Bart.

Even though she was hurt, her heart wasn't broken by her high school boyfriend who turned out to be a real rat. But something even more tragic than her father's suicide had broken Cassie Martin's heart in a million pieces, and I knew that someday she would tell me what it was.

Chapter 5
Broken Vow

ABOUT A WEEK later, Cassie and I decided to take a walk just after sunrise. Early in the morning is the only time when it's cool enough in Ohio during August to do much outside. It was worth getting up before dawn, because this year there was a special attraction. At the edge of Maple Grove where the new high school had been built, "old" Ed Hardy had planted a field of sunflowers amidst his vast acres of corn.

While walking the track at Maple Grove High School, we watched the magnificent golden blossoms that were in full bloom swaying in the breeze. What we didn't expect was the presence of the marching band. They were practicing nearby on the football field.

"Katie, I think I've found a way that I can tell you a little more about what my life is really like," Cassie said. "Over the years when I didn't have anyone to confide in, I would write about my experiences. It helped me to process what was happening more objectively."

"That sounds like journaling, which I've read can be very

beneficial in a therapeutic sort of way. In a spiritual sense, it's also a great method to record when God's at work in your life."

"The way I write is kind of like that, but it's in short story form about a specific event that actually occurred. For instance, remember when I told you that John and I were going to see Josh Groban in concert the other night?" Cassie was almost shouting now, because the band was practicing the school fight song at full volume.

"How could I forget?" I shouted back. "You were more excited than I've ever seen you since you moved here."

"Well, I wrote about it. Anyway, it's the way the evening appeared to me. Of course, I can only guess what John was really thinking or how he was feeling, so part of it might be fictional or what I prefer to term as literary license, but it helps me to observe my life as if I'm an objective outsider. It's a little strange writing about myself like I'm another person, but it clarifies my thoughts, because it can be risky for a minister's spouse to have a close friend. There are so many things that I don't feel comfortable talking about out loud, especially if anything seems even remotely critical of John. But I trust you, and I was wondering if you could read my little story. I need for someone who has had a successful marriage to give me some advice."

"Sounds fascinating, and a little complicated. I would be honored to take a look at it. You know, I love to read." As we walked back to our cars, I supportively placed my hand on Cassie's back promising, "You have my word. I won't disclose anything about it with anyone. Ever. Or about anything else that we talk about."

"I know you would never break my confidence. It's what I love about you."

When we reached her gold Camry, she retrieved the folded papers that were tucked inside her worn burgundy Bible. She handed them to me while saying, "I guess because I am the pastor's wife, women at different churches where we've served have confided about their husbands wanting to be intimate relentlessly, but without very much romantic affection being involved. These women desperately wanted to be kissed and held sometimes, without taking it to the next level. I'm sad to say one of the ladies confessed this after an affair to justify that her desperation for affection caused her to stray. My life with John isn't like that. Katie, please tell me if there are other marriages like mine."

"I'm not an expert, sweetie, but I have lived a lot longer than you. So let me give your story a read, before I say anything."

Later that same day, I closed the door to the last customer at the cafe. I poured myself a cup of coffee, sat back in my office chair, and opened the folded sheets. At the top of the white paper typed in bold black letters was the title:

Broken Vow

"John, we have to hurry or we're going to be late. The concert tickets say that the performance starts at 8 p.m., and we might not get in if we aren't there on time."

"For goodness sake, Cassie, it's only 5:30. You act like seeing Josh Groban at Blossom Music Center is the most impressive place that I've ever taken you. I'm not even the one who bought the tickets." John pulled his favorite jeans on. When he tried to fasten them, they were a bit too snug. He knew who to blame. *If Ethel Palmer doesn't stop bringing in her homemade cakes and pies when she volunteers to do the mailings, I'm not going to be able to fit into any of my clothes soon.* The spry widow had to have someone to appreciate her baking talents. Pastor John had been all too happy to oblige, but he was going to have to cut back.

While Cassie was brushing her long dark hair, she noticed her husband trying to hold his stomach in, and had to turn away so he wouldn't see how amused she was. "Why did "old" Ed Hardy give you the tickets, when it seems like his son, Ed Jr., would have liked to have gone? It's Josh Groban, and everybody likes Josh Groban."

"Why does the wealthy farmer do anything he does, Cassie? I'm sorry, if that sounded unkind, but last week after the board meeting, "old" Ed told me that we had better think long and hard, before we host another Christian concert for area youth. Having a father and son on the board is tricky. Since Ed Jr. is an accountant and our church treasurer, he told his dad exactly how much we spent in total to bring the groups in. Even though the figures were in the board notes, I guess "old" Ed hadn't added up the extra cost of security, professional lighting, and the sound company. Thankfully, the fairgrounds didn't charge us a fee other than clean-up. As far as tonight's concert, I heard Ed Jr. is buried doing some tax work for his firm right now. The tickets were probably a kind of peace offering, because even though I tried to hide it, Ed Sr. could see how frustrated I was by his criticism."

"Ed Sr. warned you about having another concert when over 2,000 teenagers turned out and heard the Gospel? No wonder you were discouraged after the board meeting." Cassie was thankful John had trusted her with this information, because he rarely opened up about any of his personal struggles with someone from the church. Apparently, it was public information though. "Old" Ed was telling anyone who would listen, he disapproved of Christian "rock" concerts. Once, Katie had to scold the meddling farmer in the coffee shop when he cornered Josh Fox, the church's youth pastor, and heatedly expressed his opinion by wagging his finger in the young minister's face.

Cassie tried to offer her exasperated spouse some sympathy while tying a beaded lime-green chiffon scarf around her neck. She untied it and draped the long sheer scarf over her shoulders. Underneath was a sleeveless ivory lace dress that accented her dark hair. She was finally pleased with her reflection in the full-length mirror. "All finished. I'm ready to go."

"You get in the car, and I'll be right there." John stopped abruptly and leaned toward his wife. For a second, she thought he was about to kiss her. Instead he turned off the light switch behind her. "You look lovely, wife of mine," he complimented her, but it sounded like an automated response. Then he hurried past her.

Cassie stood in the darkened room for a moment without moving. She could hear Katie's words ringing in her ears, "There's a little boy inside of every man" but she had no idea how to reach the man she loved. She didn't know why weeks or even months passed between the times she and John expressed any passion for each other. The busy pastor did routinely kiss her good-bye each morning when he left for church though. It was more of a habit than a soul connection. She wondered if other marriages were like this, because she knew that he loved her, and she loved him.

In the past, there had been women at whatever church they were serving who complained to her about their husbands wanting sex all the time. Not John, hardly ever, and she wasn't sure why. It hadn't always been like this, and they were still young. Something had changed in the last few years, even though everything seemed to be okay between them. He always said he was tired, and she understood that most of the time he really was exhausted. Of course, she wouldn't think of mentioning their problem to anyone else.

"Cassie, you are the one who told me we better hurry," John bellowed from the front door as he turned the porch light on. He didn't want to yell, but he was concerned she wouldn't hear him. His artistic better half was often distracted, and this caused her to run late sometimes. "We have to drive to Cuyahoga Falls and that will take at least 45 minutes, even if traffic isn't heavy."

"I'm sorry, John." *Figuring out if there was something wrong with their love life would have to wait.* "I'm on my way." She yelled back, while rushing into the living room, locking the door behind her, and following her husband outside. He was already getting into her champagne-colored Camry that was parked in the driveway. The practical minister normally drove his older well-kept Ford Ranger. The small pick-up was in immaculate condition with low mileage, and had been bequeathed to Pastor John in his uncle's will.

"Did I tell you that you look beautiful tonight, Cassie?"

"Yes, John, thank you. When you turned off the light in the bedroom a few minutes ago, you said that I looked 'lovely.'" Cassie searched her husband's face wondering if he was sincere, because even when he gave her this second compliment, he stared straight ahead. He always expressed his approval of something about her in vague terms, like it was a duty that a husband should perform. John was polite enough, but she had often heard him compliment the women in the church in the same tone of voice. That's why his words of admiration didn't make her feel too special, but she refused to let these doubts ruin their night. He was a wonderful husband, and they were on their way to see Josh Groban.

"John, you look exceptionally handsome yourself. That

light blue shirt fits you so well, and it really shows off your tan. It was on summer clearance at the Gap."

"Thanks, you're the one who bought it for me. So, I guess you get the credit. I'm constantly amazed by what a bargain shopper you are." He smiled and started the engine. They had purchased the dependable used Camry from car dealer Jay Briggs, who was also on the church board. It had been a good deal, and it was the most luxurious vehicle Cassie had ever owned. She was grateful the dealership had a service department that could be trusted to be honest when repairs were necessary. Heaven knows, John didn't have any knowledge about fixing cars even though he was a brilliant man.

He was embarrassed by his lack of mechanical aptitude, but he was a compassionate minister and inspiring preacher. His gifts were more cerebral than most men's. *Yes, my husband is probably what other people refer to as an intellectual geek,* she thought, watching him as he drove. *I don't care though; he's the best man I've ever met. So what if he can't diagnose what's wrong with a car or fix a leaky pipe?*

Other than their current lack of romance, they were the perfect couple. After the trauma she'd been through in her past, she tried to convince herself that romance and sex were overrated. She never asked questions, because she was afraid she would have to come up with some answers of her own. *Besides, real life isn't remotely like a Hallmark movie,* she scolded herself. *So much of my disenchantment and thwarted expectations stem from watching too many unrealistic chick flicks that misrepresent true love. Still...*

"Honey, I want you to know that I really appreciate all you do to minister to the emotionally wounded people at our church." John's voice broke the contemplative spell the silence had created. They had both been quiet on the drive – lost in their own thoughts. Cassie was surprised by this unexpected praise, and also by the fact they were now only miles from their destination. For a brief second, John took his eyes off the busy highway and glanced at his wife appreciatively. "I have such faith and trust in you. It astounds me that you have so much discernment and empathy when it comes to understanding brokenhearted folks, especially when you haven't experienced the kinds of tragedies they have had to deal with."

"I like to help people who are hurting by listening, because we all have hurts that only God can heal." She turned to gaze out of the passenger window. *Oh, if John only knew the truth about the tragedies I have experienced.* Cassie had grown used to concealing her secrets, so she quickly changed the subject. "John, there's the sign for our exit. We're almost there. We really are going to get to hear Josh Groban tonight!"

"Of course we're going to hear Josh Groban. It's obvious I haven't been taking you out enough, babe, at least not to the artsy affairs you're fond of. I'm sorry my schedule is so full." Her excessive excitement gave John the impression his accommodating wife might be culturally starving. He had to acknowledge their social life consisted of church potluck suppers, congregants' weddings, and occasional funeral lunches. It was obvious that his devoted helpmate, who rarely complained about anything, missed the ballet, symphony, art galleries, and eclectic restaurants, which were once part of her daily existence.

Finding a parking place wasn't nearly as bad as they had feared. Ed Hardy Sr. had included a V.I.P. parking pass with the tickets, and this perk assured them of a spot close to the entrance. Pastor John's salary wasn't conducive to a V.I.P. anything. The humble minister had to concede that it felt good to be part of this elite group for a change. It was a gorgeous late-summer evening, and when the couple entered the amphitheater, they found their seats rapidly with an usher's assistance. The Martins were so close to the stage that Cassie wouldn't even need the concert binoculars she had brought along.

John studied his spouse as if he hadn't seen her in a long time. "I'm sorry if I seem to take you for granted," he whispered in her ear. "I promise I will to try to find the time and extra money for a date to the symphony or ballet soon. I didn't realize that it's been a couple of years since we've had an opportunity to do something that you enjoy." Cassie could tell John was feeling guilty, but he was constantly overwhelmed by the demands of his position.

His father had not been an affectionate man, so he didn't know much about the little things that wives appreciate, regardless of their age. With a stoic and unromantic role model for being a husband, John couldn't guess how heartwarming an occasional bouquet of flowers or sentimental card might be to his mate.

When they were dating, he had showered Cassie with cards and flowers even if it was a single rose or a bunch of wildflowers, but that had all stopped early in their marriage. She understood this was pretty normal, as married female parishioners often complained about this to her. It hadn't concerned her until the past few years when she and her husband seemed to lose their sexual connection, too. With the stress of answering to the church board 24/7, Pastor John was consumed with implementing ways for the ministry to succeed. There wasn't any energy left over to work at his own marriage, even though he preached the importance of doing this to the couples who came to him for marital counseling.

At that moment, Josh Groban started to sing the famous song, "Broken Vow," and Cassie's eyes filled with tears. *Why is she starting to cry?* Pastor John wondered. Then when the handsome young tenor sang the words, "Who broke my faith in all these years?" he was even more confused when those tears cascaded down her cheeks.

Not tonight. Oh, please, not tonight! The ballad's lyrics had reminded the pastor's wife of the worst mistake of her life. *Will my sin never stop haunting me? It's all forgiven. Why can't I go on?* Cassie battled with the condemning thoughts swirling through her mind. The gnawing fear of what learning the truth might do to her unsuspecting spouse consumed her for a minute, until she pushed the thoughts away, as she usually did.

"Sweetie, are you all right?" John whispered, wrapping his arm protectively around her shoulder and pulling her closer to him. Since John wasn't normally affectionate in public, Cassie became instantly calm, consoled by this uncustomary chivalry. She could sense his remorse for his inability to give more of himself. She didn't believe she deserved more, so she accepted whatever he offered, concealing her desperate desire for his attention and feeling unworthy of him.

"I'm okay, John. The music is just so beautiful," she lied to cover up her guilty feelings. By then the ballad was over, and now Josh Groban was singing the very song she had hoped would be part of his repertoire that evening, "To Where You Are." The lyrics encouraged Cassie about the promise of being reunited with her dad in Heaven someday. After sharing the truth with Katie about the real cause of her father's death, she regretted that she had never had the courage to tell John about his suicide.

But it was a family secret, and she had kept it from her husband for so long, that it seemed too late to tell him the true story. Besides, only those who have had a loved one take their own life can fully comprehend what suicide does to those left behind. There's the self-blame or blaming others, the guilt, the anger, and the grieving of what might have been. On the occasions when someone in their church lost someone to suicide, Cassie desperately wanted to console them by saying, "I really do understand." Instead she hid her pain, and no one – not even her husband – suspected that she had experienced this tragedy firsthand. She was relieved that Katie knew now. Having this wonderful woman as a spiritual mother was such a blessing.

John heard his wife's deep sigh, and felt her tense body relax. He continued to hold her close as they listened to the poignant lyrics that brought such comfort to those grieving. Pastor John had heard the song sung at many of the funerals he had conducted in the past fifteen years, but he never grew tired of it. "Fly me up to where you are beyond the distant star. I wish upon tonight to see you smile...a breath away is not too far to where you are."

Without thinking about who was watching or that he was a minister, Pastor John kissed Cassie, a long lingering kiss, and she kissed him back. Although after the drive home when the concert was over, the exhausted clergyman began snoring before Cassie could even climb into her side of their queen-size bed.

Cassie was too excited to sleep. She thanked God for Josh Groban's beautiful music and for the moment of closeness she and her husband had experienced that night. Her father's death had taught her to never take anything for granted, and instead of wondering why there weren't more moments like the one during the concert, she drifted off into a deep sleep grateful for an evening she would remember forever.

When I finished reading the heartrending account, I was more confused than ever. Not only didn't I have an explanation for why Pastor John might not be more interested in being with Cassie sexually, but where was all this guilt on her part coming from? Jake and I had such an uncomplicated intimate relationship, because we had never been with anyone else. It was just us for all those years, and thankfully, we had both kept our marriage vows.

Had Cassie been unfaithful to Pastor John at some point in the past? Did her husband suspect this betrayal? Is that why it was difficult for him to feel close to her? Could it have something to do with the fact that they weren't able to have children? Even worse, what if our poor pastor was battling a pornography issue? I had read that a lot of men, including those in ministry, were involved in Internet pornography or maybe he really was tired all the time?

What will I tell Cassie when she asks for my opinion? My goodness, I think I am in way over my head on this one. I didn't realize that some married couples lead such a sexless existence. When they're older that can happen, but Cassie and Pastor John are relatively young. Well, young by my standards that is.

I'll have to refer my pastor's wife to Dr. Jasmine Jones, Lizzie's granddaughter, for a little confidential advice. As a psychologist and trained family therapist, I'll bet she will be able to shed some light on the situation. Or maybe Jasmine will refer the couple to a physician if it's a medical problem, because sometimes even pastors need a little bit of help.

Chapter 6
A Gatsby Look-Alike

CASSIE LOOKED ESPECIALLY stunning that destiny-filled Tuesday in early October when she stopped in for a latte. She was wearing a knee-length, black, tunic sweater dress with matching tights and black leather ankle boots, which silhouetted her slender shape.

Her accessories included an expensive-looking watch, which wasn't expensive at all, and earrings that sparkled like diamonds but were really cubic zirconium. A pastor's salary and her meager art commissions didn't allow for real diamonds.

Cassie had been thrilled when she bought those trendy boots at a Cleveland Goodwill Store. "I feel like God blessed me with these boots," she gushed excitedly, showing me her thrift store find. "I couldn't possibly have afforded real leather, and they are black, just the color I wanted." The minister's wife was silent for a minute rubbing her hand almost lovingly down the side of one of the boots she was wearing.

"Boy, you sure seem like you are happy about something,

Cassie girl." Since she hadn't mentioned anything about her story of the Josh Groban concert, I decided that I was not going to bring it up until she did. The topic of sex was probably something that neither of us was quite ready to discuss. Writing about something is one thing, but talking about it is entirely another.

"Do you think God cares about whether I have new boots, Katie?" She didn't give me time to reply. Instead, she answered herself, "I do. That's how I see Him as a father. It's not that we always get what we want, but sometimes I glimpse God's goodness in little things like these leather boots." This is what made me love my spiritual daughter so much. Her kind heart was filled with gratitude for the simple gifts in life, which other people often took for granted.

Besides being grateful for what she had, Cassie was always trying to stretch their tight budget. I had learned that on Tuesday mornings she would dress up and drive to Cleveland to the art gallery where she occasionally sold a painting. Unfortunately, her watercolors didn't sell as often as she let others believe.

Not wanting her husband to feel overwhelmed by their lack of finances, she found another way to make extra money. No one would have suspected that the industrious woman was a vintage dealer of sorts. Wherever the couple lived, Cassie would search for small artsy and antique objects at local thrift stores and garage sales and then sell them on consignment or occasionally on eBay. After they moved to Maple Grove, she started consigning a few items each week at an upscale Cleveland store. Vintage jewelry was her specialty. The shop's owner, Maggie Bryan, liked the resourceful pastor's wife who, with her museum background, brought in some pretty amazing antique and shabby-chic pieces for her to resell.

"Why don't you tell Pastor John that you sell items through the Cleveland store?" I once asked Cassie. "It seems to me, your husband would be proud of the creative way you make much-needed income." Even though this appeared to be a harmless omission, I was concerned Cassie's behavior represented her inability to trust her husband with more significant secrets.

"Oh, no, Katie." Cassie seemed shocked by my suggestion. "I can't tell him. He would feel like he doesn't provide adequately for us. It's my way of helping out. I don't have to ask him for anything, because he thinks the proceeds from my paintings keep me in spending money. Maybe it's my pride, too, because I've never become a successful artist."

Despite the Martins' restrictive budget, there were a few church gossips who made snide comments about Cassie wearing expensive jewelry when people in our community were going to bed hungry at night. I didn't mention these busybodies or their untrue statements, but she sensed their disapproval. After being a pastor's wife for more than 15 years, she had learned that she couldn't win when it came to pleasing everyone. A long time ago, she'd given up trying. Still, she was wounded by the hurtful words and judgment of others.

It wasn't Cassie's fault she made everything, even a cheap rhinestone watch and CZ earrings, look elegant. Dressed in her black outfit that Tuesday, she appeared every inch the accomplished artist, even though her paintings sold infrequently and for not much money.

"Today's the day, Katie," Cassie said with both determination and resignation in her voice.

"What day?" I replied nonchalantly while writing tomorrow's breakfast special on the dry-erase menu board.

As Cassie stood in the front picture window of Katie's Coffee Corner, the afternoon sun illuminated the auburn highlights in her brunette hair. Her face was framed by a background of autumn's breathtaking crimson leaves from the maple trees outside the shop.

"Katie, I came later than usual because I know that you have a little quiet time in the coffee shop about now. This is the day. I have to tell you the rest of the story. The truth about who the pastor's wife really is."

I could tell that this might be more than I wanted to know. But Cassie had to trust someone in order to get this emotional weight she carried off her pretty shoulders. And for some reason, she trusted me. "Sounds like a latte day, Cassie girl. Let me make you one. Then we'll settle in for a chat."

Cassie did trust me. For the past year, she had shared confidences with me. At first, she'd tested the waters with meaningless information. Before long, she'd begun to rest implicitly in my confidentiality. Eventually, she'd trusted me with the deepest and darkest secrets of her life. Today, she would divulge a truth that she feared would make me view her differently. She had to tell someone. She couldn't bear the emotional weight of her secret anymore.

"Since I have Brianna working late this afternoon, why don't you and I let her handle things in here? We can go sit outside on the bench in the back and enjoy this gorgeous day."

Brianna Walker is a college junior who works part-time. Normally, I wouldn't leave her in the shop alone, since she's only been a barista a few months. With the police station two doors down, security isn't the issue. The problem is she gets flustered when folks line up to order specialty coffee drinks. She confuses the recipes and customers complain. But the day had been unusually slow. I detected what Cassie was about to tell me was important enough for me to take a break. Plus, I'd be out back if Brianna needed help.

Cassie and I sat on the wooden bench together. She slowly and carefully blew on the white frothy foam of her steaming latte trying to gather the courage to talk about the circumstances which had almost destroyed her. I could discern this much from her distressed expression.

"Could I say a little prayer, Cassie? Maybe that would help you get started."

Cassie eagerly nodded. "Yes."

"Dear Lord, please send your Holy Spirit to be with us in a special way today. My spiritual daughter needs your grace and courage to reveal the secret that has been keeping her imprisoned in her past. Please, let her have the assurance she can trust me with the truth, no matter how terrible she thinks that truth is, because I couldn't love her more if she were my own child. Give her peace in accepting that there is no brokenness which you cannot heal or youthful sin that you will not forgive in Jesus' name."

"Amen," Cassie said sounding relieved. Then she dove right in. "Remember when I told you I vowed never to let a man get close to me when my father died, because I was terrified of being abandoned again? Well, unfortunately, I broke my promise to myself, with a man who shattered my heart into a million little pieces."

She looked at me intently, about to disclose the reality of the heartbreak from which she hadn't fully recovered. A look of anguish flooded her heart-shaped face, and tears filled her hazel eyes. "No matter what you tell me, I am not going to judge you, Cassie. I can promise you that, because God knows I haven't been a perfect human being. No one has ever been perfect, except our Savior."

"Okay, Katie," she sighed with resignation. "It all began when I met Jon Blevins my junior year of college, while I was studying at the University of the Arts in Philadelphia. Initially, Jon seemed like an incredibly charming and knowledgeable instructor. He might have the same name as my wonderful husband, John, but nothing else about these two men is remotely similar. Even the spelling of my instructor's name was different, since it was J-O-N. Later, I even wondered if Jon was his real name, or if that was fictitious like everything else.

"Anyway, Jon Blevins taught creative writing at the

77

university, and I was very excited about taking his course." Cassie cleared her throat and looked down for a moment composing herself.

"Jon wasn't really on staff there. He was an adjunct faculty member who was supplementing his income while finishing the great American novel that he said would rival F. Scott Fitzgerald's *The Great Gatsby*." Cassie had a tone of disgust in her voice when she said this. She was still angry at herself for being naïve and also angry at the man who had wounded her deeply.

"When I was a teenager, I'd read and reread Fitzgerald's classic novel. On the first day of class, when Jon Blevins introduced himself, he asked if any of us had read it. I remember how proud I felt when I raised my hand. About half of the forty students in the class also raised their hands, but Dr. Jon Blevins looked directly at me when he said, 'If you liked *The Great Gatsby*, you will definitely enjoy this class. I can promise you that.' Then he winked at me. Oh, Katie, I was such a foolish young woman back then." She paused, as if she couldn't go on.

"What happened after you met him?" I asked, trying to encourage her. "If you are going to start feeling better about yourself, the only way is to get it all out."

"When Jon looked at me that first day of class, I should have run the other way. Instead, I felt flattered, and my heart pounded so hard I thought my chest would burst. Then I smiled back at him." The minister's wife blushed. Her cheeks turned bright red recalling her passionate reaction to Jon's attention.

"I couldn't help but notice how remarkably Jon's appearance resembled that of Jay Gatsby, the main character in Fitzgerald's novel. My attractive instructor was the picture of aristocracy in his stylish blazer, tailored shirt, and pleated pants, and I fell for it. Also like Gatsby, who acquired his fortune through his involvement with organized crime, my married professor lacked the personal character necessary to be a man of integrity. Despite his mysterious financial dealings, a misguided Gatsby did remain dedicated to Daisy, the married woman he loved. Jon Blevins, on the other hand, was only dedicated to bolstering his own ego through the co-ed conquests he made on the campus, and sadly I become one of them."

I tried not to react, understanding that to an inexperienced young woman, her English professor had appeared a fascinating and sophisticated man of the world.

"I was swept off my feet by the attention of a man who was so unlike the boys I had dated. Often, he would ask me to stay after class for a few minutes to discuss my latest paper." Cassie dropped her head again, but this time she covered her face with her hands and began to cry openly. "Then, one day he asked me if I would like to go for a cup of coffee, explaining that he would appreciate my input about the novel he was working on."

She reached down for the latte I had made for her. She picked it up from off the spot in the lawn where she had set it close to the bench. The minister's wife clasped the mug tightly in both of her hands as if it were the culprit that had caused all the trouble.

"Deep within, a warning siren sounded loudly, telling me that my handsome English professor was crossing the line of appropriate behavior. But, I didn't listen, because I was overwhelmed by my desire to impress him."

Cassie didn't offer any excuses. "I knew it was wrong to spend time with a married man." It was the same old story. "Jon continually told me that he and his wife were no longer in love, and they were only staying together for the sake of their children. He said they were going to divorce soon."

Besides the innocence of youth, Cassie's spiritual compass was almost nonexistent by the time she met Blevins during college. Although she had become a believer as a child, that long-ago commitment must have seemed like a distant memory as a troubled teenager. After her father's suicide, the "Why?" question had strangled the seeds of faith that had once been sprouting in her young heart.

One afternoon in the coffee shop she'd explained, "As well as causing me to question my own faith, when my dad took his life, no one from our church reached out to us. It was as if my father had committed a terrible sin, rather than folks having compassion for his struggle with a mental health issue. I even overheard a lady from church tell Mom that what my father had done was 'weak and selfish.' Don't think I'm trying to make excuses, but my mother and I desperately needed to be loved and accepted. In a way, we were shunned.

People acted almost afraid that the calamity that happened to us might be catching, fearful that it could happen to them."

I remember being surprised by this revelation, making Cassie more intense as she continued, "There aren't any words to express how horrendously suicide affects the loved ones left behind, especially if no one talks about it. After the initial shock of my dad's death, and everyone in my family blaming themselves, we just locked it away and never mentioned the taboo subject again."

For a few seconds I contemplated how the young girl and her mother might have felt abandoned by God's people during a time of such immense loss. But that conversation had happened months ago.

"Katie, am I upsetting you?"

When I heard the concern in Cassie's voice, I was jarred back into the present. I also realized the hard bench was starting to feel uncomfortable. "I'm so sorry for being distracted. Of course you aren't upsetting me. I was just thinking about something you told me a couple of months ago, about your father's suicide. Spiritually, you didn't have any support system after that incident, because your church failed you when you needed it most. This was one of the factors that left you vulnerable to Jon Blevins' attention."

When I mentioned her dad's death, I saw a haunted look of unhealed grieving that probably transported her back to that awful night in the garage. Someday, this girl was going to get better. I reached for her and hugged her closely to me.

Cassie pulled away, saying, "There was also this religious

legalism that ultimately strangled any desire I had to attend church, or even to try to make good decisions. This all came to a climax about the same time I met Jon. I gave up on God, and then Jon appeared out of nowhere. For a while, he became like a god to me."

She was tired of trying to do things the right way, so she decided to see what it was like to break the rules. The first innocent cup of coffee she had with her manipulative instructor opened a door to the heartache that would follow her for two decades.

"I won't draw this out, Katie, and I'm not making excuses for what I did. It was terribly wrong, but I want you to understand how I fell for Jon."

My sympathetic smile urged her on.

"Jon Blevins was the most charismatic man I had ever met. I was so hungry for the attention of a man like him, who seemed to be everything my father urged me to wait for. I just knew that he was my prince."

Cassie shook her head in disgust, ashamed of how naïve she had been. "He was married, Katie, and he had little children. I disregarded all that to chase my romantic fantasy of who he seemed to be, not who he really was."

Chapter 7
A Tragic Tale of Innocence Lost

SLOWLY, THE SAD story came out. Cassie met her professor for coffee a few times, and they discussed his novel and her dream of being an artist. Jon listened to Cassie as no man had ever listened before. He assured her she could be anything she wanted to be. Then he asked her to supper. They went to an expensive restaurant in an exclusive Philadelphia hotel, where the waiter asked if they would like to share a bottle of wine. Cassie began to say, "No," since she had never consumed alcohol before. But Jon insisted they have wine to celebrate their first evening together. Jon's insistence made Cassie feel like an inexperienced school girl. She didn't want to tell him about her late father's addiction resulting in her decision to abstain from alcoholic beverages. She was too afraid it would dampen the mood of the most romantic evening she had ever experienced.

"Jon asked for the wine list, and I just sat there, feeling intoxicated by being close to him. If I would have said, 'No,' that night might have ended differently. When the wine arrived, Jon poured me a glass, filled his own goblet, and then toasted to 'Our first evening together.'

"The syrupy red liquid tasted bitter initially, almost medicinal. After the first glass, the second went down easier. The wine made me feel lightheaded, as if I didn't have a care in the world. By the time the bottle was gone, I was feeling more uninhibited than I'd ever felt."

"Let's order another bottle?" Jon suggested innocently.

"'I really shouldn't...' I began to reply, but before I could finish Jon called the waiter over. The second bottle arrived, and when we were halfway through it, Jon and I shared a passionate kiss at our table."

Cassie downed the last of her now-cold latte plunging ahead with the terrible tale, fearing that if she didn't get it out, she would never tell anyone.

"Jon had the whole thing planned. I'm sure he had used this routine on other girls. He said we shouldn't be kissing publicly, because he didn't want me to be embarrassed later. He sounded downright chivalrous when he offered, 'Cassie, I already have a room here. I thought I would stay the night instead of going back to the suburbs. Darling, I know you have had too much wine. Why don't you come to my room and lie down for a bit before I take you back to your apartment?'"

Cassie rented an apartment near campus with three other coeds. She hadn't breathed a word about her date with Jon Blevins, fearing what her roommates might think. She knew she was in no condition to go home just then.

"Foolishly, playing right into Jon's trap, I agreed to go to his room, saying, 'Jon, I do think I need to take a little nap. It would be nice to lie down.' I recall having trouble getting my words out. They were all slurring together. The wine had numbed my senses, and I was so drunk that I had to lean heavily on him to make it to his hotel room."

Sympathetically, I shook my head at her confession, not wanting to hear what I dreaded would come next. I thought it was divine providence that Brianna, my young barista, hadn't interrupted our conversation needing my help in the cafe.

"I guess there's no reason to go into the sordid details of what happened. On the way up to that room, I was a virgin. The following morning, when I was leaving the hotel with Jon, I was hung over, confused, and ashamed because I had given away something that I had been saving all my life for my prince."

I just nodded, knowing in advance how the clandestine supper was going to end. "Go on, sweetie. Get it all out. You'll feel better."

"Jon didn't even drive me all the way home, Katie. He dropped me off a block from my apartment, saying he didn't want me to be self-conscious in front of my friends. I'd like to tell you that I didn't see him after that night. But, that night was only the beginning of a year-long affair. Jon and I would meet in a coffee shop, a library, but most often, we would end up together late at night in his locked office."

Cassie stood and stretched. Then she pulled a red leaf off of a nearby maple tree and began methodically to rip it apart. "It was wrong, but my desire for Jon blinded me to everything I had once believed was right. For the first time since my father died, I felt I had a man in my life who adored me. Jon always told me that as soon as he could leave his wife, he would. Then, accidentally, I bumped into Joyce Blevins one day in his office, and I realized that Jon had been lying to me all along, but by then it was too late."

The pastor's wife sat back on the bench, buried her face in her hands, and began sobbing. "How could I have done that? How could I?"

I patted Cassie's back while she cried. I wasn't a trained counselor, but anyone could see the weighty emotional price this disclosure had cost her. "Maybe you've shared enough for one day. I don't want you to upset yourself...."

"No." Cassie cut me off. "If I don't tell you today, I might not ever tell anyone." She took a deep breath and looked right at me when she said with horror in her voice, "His wife was obviously pregnant with another child, and although Jon didn't know it, so was I."

This was not a part of the story I had expected. I bit my lower lip hard, but I couldn't hide my shock. *Where was Cassie's child?* I decided not to interrupt her with my questions, and just to let the awful account pour out of her, hoping to purge her of the past.

Instantly, Cassie became strangely calm. A tormented look twisted the sides of her mouth, and tears silently cascaded down her cheeks. "Joyce came to Jon's office that afternoon to bring him his briefcase. He had forgotten it in the morning. She wasn't at all the unkempt nag he had told me about. Rather, she was a pretty, blonde, thirty-something woman who was lovingly holding the hand of an also blonde little girl about four years old. She was well into her third trimester of pregnancy, a fact I hadn't known, and a red-haired boy of about six protectively stood on her other side. I started to walk into Jon's office, but then I saw his family gathered around him.

"Unaware of my presence, when Joyce told Jon that she would see him that night, he affectionately patted her round belly and teased, 'I'll see both of you when I get home.' Then he kissed her the way a doting husband kisses his pregnant wife before she walked out the back door of his office. At that moment my illusion of Jon Blevins as a charming prince was shattered. Not only was Jon not a prince, but he was the worst kind of man: a man who cheated on a wife who had great love and trust for him. The look of adoration in Joyce Blevins' eyes couldn't be denied. She looked at him as I had, until that very moment. Jon turned and was momentarily startled when he saw me standing in the hallway just outside."

I couldn't help interrupting, shocked by the scope of this deception. "Oh, Cassie, that must have been terrible for you. What a betrayal for both you and his wife. What did Jon do then?"

Cassie wiped fresh tears from her eyes. "He quickly regained his composure, hoping that I had not witnessed the intimate scene with his family. 'Dear Cassie, where have you been all my life?' he said, smiling that appealing smile that normally melted my heart. This time it sickened me, realizing the truth about who he really was.

"When he held his arms out to me, I began to run so fast in the other direction that there was no way he would be able to catch up with me. It was winter, and there was ice and snow outside. Despite the freezing temperatures, I didn't even take time to put my coat back on. I just left it hanging on the coat rack in the office's waiting room."

For a moment, there was silence. Then the pastor's wife confessed, "I had gone there to tell Jon about the baby. I had thought he would be so pleased that I was giving him a reason to leave the dreadful woman who chained him to her with his children. After I saw Joyce, I knew she wasn't the despicable one. It was Jon who was a liar and a cheat."

Where is the child? The thought kept racing through my mind. I wondered if Pastor John Martin knew any of this tragic tale.

"I ran so fast that soon I found myself almost three blocks from Jon's office in a deserted area of the campus. Not paying attention to my surroundings, while running, I hit a patch of black ice and slipped and fell so hard that I was knocked unconscious. When I woke up, I was in a hospital bed with a concerned-looking nurse standing over me.

"'You're back among the living!' the nurse said a little too brightly. Groggily, I asked the overly cheerful R.N. what had happened, feeling as if I had been run over by a truck. 'You took a terrible tumble on the ice, but you're going to be just fine,' she replied in a guarded voice that let me know everything was not going to be fine.

"'My baby?' I couldn't believe that I had said those words out loud. It was not Jon's baby anymore, just mine. I had always wanted to be a mother, admittedly not a single one though. Anyway, there hadn't been time to think the circumstances through. Sadly, I might have considered abortion if I would have contemplated motherhood alone, or being linked to Jon forever. I was lost, desperate, and making such poor choices back then, I'm ashamed to say an abortion might have seemed like a solution, and I would have that awful guilt to deal with too.

"Instead when I saw the nurse's sad look, I knew there was no longer an infant to be concerned about. She tried to dodge the truth. 'Let's wait until the doctor comes to talk about the effects of your accident.'

"For the next few hours, I twisted my hurting body into fetal position and folded my hands over my now-empty belly consumed with grief. Had I angered God so badly that He took my child, or was it an accident as the nurse had said? I also felt guilty for being filled with a tremendous sense of relief that I wouldn't have to be connected to a man like Jon Blevins for one more day.

"When the physician finally came in late that night, he expressed his sympathy for my loss. 'I'm very sorry, but you experienced a miscarriage. It appears you were about three months along.'

"I was surprised, because I had only found out the week

before from a home pregnancy test that I was expecting. I had been suspicious for more than a month though, when my favorite foods were making me queasy. I took the test twice to make sure the results were accurate. My cycle had always been irregular, so I had no idea how far along I was. Somehow this information made everything seem worse.

"The physician continued, 'You fell so hard, the impact caused great trauma. Fortunately, a student who was passing by witnessed your accident. He called 911 when he saw that you were unconscious. You lost quite a bit of blood when you miscarried. From the wallet in your purse, we were able to identify you, Miss Kirk.'

"The doctor tried to be professional. 'Thankfully, you were spared a head injury, and you didn't break any bones. But your knees are badly bruised, and your hands are pretty scraped up from breaking your fall.' He didn't ask any questions other than, 'Is there someone we can call for you? You should be able to be discharged in the morning.'

"'No, there isn't anyone,' I said looking down at my hospital gown so that the doctor wouldn't see my tears mingled with rage at my deceptive lover and at myself. In that moment I made a silent promise never to speak to Jon Blevins again, other than to tell him I was through with him. As for my mother and roommates, I could only hope that none of them would ever learn about my sordid affair.

"I expected the physician, who looked rather ominous in his starched white coat, would leave and let me mourn my loss. Instead, he sat in the chair at the end of my bed. *What other information could he have?* 'Is there something else I should know, Doctor?'

"'I'm afraid, Miss Kirk, I have more bad news.' He cleared his throat. 'Truthfully, your pregnancy was highly unusual, as you are suffering from a disease known as endometriosis. In your case, it is quite severe. I'm surprised you haven't been treated for pelvic discomfort and painful menstruation. I'm sorry, but I do not think it will be at all likely that you will ever conceive again. However, because you were able to get pregnant this time, there is a slight chance.'

"'Doctor, are you telling me that I might not be able to have children?' I was beyond grief-stricken. I had lost a baby, and was now being told there might not be any future children. I didn't bother to tell the physician I had been taking pain medication for the exact symptoms he described.

"'I am sorry, but there is that possibility. Surgery is an option, but we can't assure you it would be successful. For the present, you need to recover before you even worry about this matter.'

"'Thank you, Doctor. I do understand.' I silently accepted what I believed was my punishment for loving someone who didn't belong to me. I slept fitfully that night in the hospital. The next morning after I was discharged, I took a taxi to my apartment. Then I wrote Jon Blevins a letter telling him what I witnessed in his office and how I didn't want to see him again for as long as I lived.

"Jon left messages on my answering machine for a couple of weeks after he received the letter. But I didn't return his phone calls or ever tell him about the baby we had lost." Cassie rose from the bench where she had sat for the past hour. "I didn't think Jon deserved to know we almost had a child together, Katie. It wasn't long before he stopped calling."

Slowly, I stood from the bench, too, and wiped a few remaining tears from Cassie's cheeks with my wrinkled hand. Her eyes were red and swollen, and I was sure she had cried herself completely out of tears. Cassie seemed oblivious to my touch, with her thoughts still centered on her painful past of two decades ago. She smiled wryly.

"I heard rumors that Jon was seeing a sophomore who was in the class he taught about Jane Austen's novels." The pastor's wife was spent now that her secret had been disclosed. She looked as if a hundred-pound weight had been lifted from her.

"Cassie, I'm so sorry that you have suffered all this, but I'm thankful you trust me enough to share your heartbreak with me." I put my arms around her like someone would embrace a hurting little girl. "I always sensed tragedy about you, but I had no idea just how tragic. We all make poor choices, dear child, and I think you have suffered quite enough. Does your husband know about the baby you lost?"

"He could never look at me the same way if he knew all this. He doesn't know about the baby, or Jon, or even my father's suicide." Not waiting for my reaction, my minister's wife grabbed her purse and started walking away rapidly, as if she was trying to run from the secret she had just told me. Trying to erase the horrible truth of the past by changing the subject, Cassie called over her shoulder, "Next time, I'll tell you the romantic story of how my husband and I met, Katie. For now, I have to get home and start supper."

Absorbed in Cassie's harrowing account, I hadn't observed the pleasant Indian summer afternoon's bright sunshine and crystal-clear blue skies turn overcast. As the temperature dropped dramatically, fall's coolness invaded the air.

Without the sun's golden rays shining through the maple trees, their glowing crimson leaves dimmed to an opaque ruby red. Still, my mind was flooded with the light of God's glory and my heart was warmed with gratitude for His restoring grace. My spiritual daughter was on her way to breaking free. While grasping the doorknob to the back entrance of my coffeehouse, I paused to bow my head in silent thanks.

Chapter 8
A Match Made in Heaven

CASSIE DIDN'T COME into my coffee shop the following week. I think she wanted to have time to herself after telling me the details of her love affair with Jon Blevins. It wasn't as if she were mentally ill and needed a psychiatrist; she simply needed a friend. Although I suppose guilt can jeopardize your mental health if you carry it around as long as Cassie had. I was thankful I was the one she chose to share her confidences with. I had longed for a daughter's companionship, and she had yearned for an authentic sister-in-the-faith who would care about her as an individual, not about her position as the pastor's wife.

Even with her unseen trials, it isn't exaggerating to say Cassie ministered to the congregants of Maple Avenue Community Church in a powerful way. I marveled at how church members trusted her with their private issues right from the beginning. I told her a lot of my secrets too, since most everyone has hidden heartbreak. It seems broken people can instantly spot another person whose heart has been crushed by adversity.

Yet no one in our fellowship would imagine the misery Cassie Martin had encountered. Her non-judgmental attitude prompted folks to flock to her for support and a listening ear. For serious situations, she urged people to consult with either her husband, Pastor Ginger Graham, or Pastor Ron Jacobs.

Bringing 32-year-old Rev. Graham on staff part-time was one of John Martin's first accomplishments. M.A.C. church had never had a female minister before. Ed Hardy Sr. and Ed Jr. disagreed over Pastor Ginger's placement, in spite of her willingness to accept two-thirds of the weekly wages her male counterparts required. In the end, her background and academic credentials were so exemplary, "old" Ed lost the battle.

As for Cassie's compassion, because of her ability to uplift others, rarely did anyone inquire about her welfare. For instance, finances weren't easy for the couple. Like many rural churches, Maple Avenue didn't offer a big salary, despite the lead pastor's weighty responsibilities. The parsonage was supposed to make up for what was lacking in his paycheck. Preparing for the future, they were wise stewards saving every extra penny to one day purchase a home of their own.

Cassie's meager income also helped with their budget, but there was no money for extras. I never heard the pastor's wife complain, and she was always grateful for what anyone gave her. That's why, whenever I could legitimately get away with giving the Martins a present for a birthday, anniversary,

Pastor Appreciation week, or Christmas, my blessing would be a gift card for Katie's Coffee Corner. Then, if Cassie or Pastor John wanted a latte, muffin, piece of homemade pie, or one of my famous Rueben sandwiches, they could have it.

The following week though, rather than meeting at my cafe, Cassie invited me to the parsonage while Pastor John was visiting a seriously ill parishioner who had undergone heart surgery at the Cleveland Clinic. This invitation was another sign of her growing trust, because she rarely had guests in her home. She often referred to it as their "little haven."

"You promised to tell me how you met your husband, Cassie." Grabbing a homemade brownie from a plate of assorted cookies setting on the table, I gazed around their cozy home. Every nook and cranny portrayed her artistic touch. There were twinkling lights tastefully adorning the kitchen border she created by painting delicate wildflowers. Scented candles were lit, and autumn's multi-colored mums were arranged in an antique, cobalt-glass vase in the center of the early 1900s oak table.

"Well, Katie, senior year of college, I did an internship at the Philadelphia Museum of Art. Following graduation, they asked me to stay on in a paid position as the assistant director of volunteers. On a couple of occasions, late at night, museum security found me asleep at my desk in my office, collapsed after an exhausting day. After my relationship with my English professor ended, I maintained a relentlessly hectic schedule, organizing the museum docents and volunteers to excuse my noticeably absent social life.

"One of the museum accountants was a woman in her mid-forties named Gioletta DeMarco. Gigi, as she was affectionately called by most of the staff, was a very perceptive and caring lady who wasn't fooled by my adamant protest that I didn't have time to have friends or to date. Gigi quickly figured out that I wasn't too busy, but too afraid to let others in."

Cassie walked around her kitchen, stopping to check the tea kettle on the stove. "She had maternal instincts like you, Katie, and she wondered what had happened to make me so terrified of relationships. Whatever the problem was, Gigi thought that a good church might be the answer to provide some support for me. Therefore, with a nurturing mother's determination, she occasionally invited me to her fellowship for special events.

"So, that's how it all started. Late one Friday afternoon, when the museum office staff was preparing to leave for the weekend, Gigi asked me if I was busy on Sunday morning. Besides being an accountant, Gigi was also a talented musician who was going to be singing her own arrangement of *Amazing Grace* that morning. She explained that her congregation was having a special service celebrating the ordination of a seminarian who was a nephew of their pastor."

The tea kettle began whistling. Cassie removed it from the burner and filled a hand-painted china teapot that had been her grandmother's to the brim with the boiling water. Then she added three bags of ginger peach tea.

While the tea steeped, she continued. "I didn't really have any interest in visiting Gigi's church, because I had dutifully attended church while growing up – before my father's suicide – and found nothing there except rigid laws that seemed impossible to keep. After my affair with Jon and the accident that caused me to lose my baby, I feared that my self-fulfilling prophecy of being a hopeless lawbreaker had come to pass. I suspected I would find nothing but more condemnation and guilt in a church."

Cassie set the pot on the table, and I poured the hot tea into hand-painted cups that matched the teapot. "I genuinely cared about Gigi's feelings. She had been kind to me during my early days at the museum, when my life was filled with chaos because of my clandestine meetings with Jon. After we broke up and I lost the baby, Gigi didn't know what was wrong, but she sensed my distress. She kept inviting me to lunch and reaching out to me any way that she could."

"Please, tell me more about Gigi. She sounds like she was a blessing from God at that point in your life. By the way, these are delicious." I grabbed another brownie off the plate.

Cassie took a cautious sip of her tea, making sure it wasn't too hot. "Gigi wasn't pushy, so she didn't ask me to church too often – only when she sensed the frightening aloneness, which I tried my best to hide. This time, when Gigi invited me to her fellowship, before I could stop myself, it was as if the words involuntarily rolled off my tongue, 'You're singing? Of course, I would enjoy coming on Sunday morning.'"

Cassie laughed out loud now. Her hazel eyes sparkled as she remembered. "What was I saying, 'Enjoy coming?' I was instantly terrified that I might have made a poor decision to accept Gigi's invitation." Then she looked serious again. "But the dark depression was once again swallowing me up, and I couldn't bear to be alone with it. I could function okay during my waking hours at the museum, but during the night, a gripping fear would often awaken me. I would find myself soaked with perspiration, immobilized by icy terror. It had been this way for me since the accident. In my mind, that is the way I always refer to losing my baby: 'the accident.'

"That's why I reassured myself that it would be okay to visit Gigi's church that Sunday. I reasoned that it might even do me some good to spend time around other people. As far as the service itself, I made a vow to guard my emotions and not allow my already low self-esteem to be further decimated by legalistic preaching. I knew I was a wretched sinner, but I had no idea I could be forgiven.

"That Sunday, I woke up before the alarm clock even went off. I was nervous because I would be meeting Gigi's family, so I wanted to look just right. *Err on the side of conservative,* I inwardly cautioned myself as I looked through my closet. Then I saw the perfect outfit: a navy blue two-piece suit."

"You wore a navy blue suit to visit a church? Sounds more like a job interview." I chuckled as I teased Cassie, because

I always dress casually, even on Sundays. In confirmation, I straightened my faded blue jeans.

Cassie giggled. "This was almost twenty years ago, Katie. Most women didn't wear pants to church. Dresses and suits were popular in a city like Philadelphia. If someone had shown up in jeans, or even worse, leggings, they would have been the talk of the congregation, and not in a good way. We've come a long way in our flexibility to wear casual clothes to Sunday services, but I still like to dress up.

"Besides, that morning I intuitively felt that my life was about to change dramatically. I took a long hot shower and dressed in the navy blue suit, accessorizing with navy pumps and a delicate pearl necklace. I was cautious about how much makeup I wore. I highlighted my eyes with a little brown liner. Curled my waist-length hair with a curling iron and let it hang loose. Then I completed my outfit with a touch of pale pink lipstick and pearl stud earrings."

Cassie's brownish green eyes flashed with intensity. "Katie, I vividly recall every detail of my preparation that morning. It was as if I was Esther of the Old Testament preparing to be presented to the king for his approval. I know it sounds kind of spooky spiritual, but I really did sense that somehow my life was going to change forever. The artist inside of me, the one who rarely had an opportunity to paint in those days, enjoyed this ritual of dressing. Of course, I didn't know I was about to meet my own prince."

I stood and looked closely at a picture of a field of yellow daffodils that Cassie had painted. "Why didn't you paint,

Cassie? Wouldn't your artwork have been therapeutic in helping you heal from your heartbreak?"

"It's strange, but when I worked at the museum I didn't have much opportunity to paint. My schedule was too hectic. But, when you're artistic, it manifests in all kind of ways."

Cassie poured me another cup of tea, then filled her own cup. "You are right, though. After my college heartbreak, it was my artistic nature that seemed to save me from total emotional annihilation. I would feel almost dead inside, but then I would go to work at the museum. Just being around the magnificent paintings, sculptures, and glasswork would rekindle my passion for color, symmetry, and creative expression."

I sat down again and took another sip of tea. "Well, tell me more about that morning you met Pastor John."

"All right, after I finished dressing, when I glanced in the mirror one last time, I almost believed I was who I saw there: a successful professional female with my whole future before me. This was a far cry from my almost constant reality of being an emotionally broken young woman stuck in the past.

"I drove to the Fairview Community Church which was nestled in a quiet Philadelphia suburb about a half an hour from where I lived. When I pulled my Honda Civic into the packed parking lot, I panicked momentarily. Gigi hadn't told me that her church was so large. I thought, *Oh well, it's easier to get lost in a crowd.* This thought instantly calmed my fears.

"I leisurely strolled through the parked cars, realizing that I was almost twenty minutes early for the 10:30 a.m. service.

How will I ever find Gigi in this crowd? I wondered as people hurried past me. Just then, a parking lot greeter with the nametag, "Marcus," pinned to his suit jacket shouted, 'Good morning, young lady! Can I be of assistance in helping you to find your way?'

"Marcus's warm smile assured me that things were okay. I answered, 'No. I'm just on my way inside to find a friend.'

"When I reached the church's entrance doors, a vivacious, middle-aged woman asked, 'How are you this morning?' The attractive blonde detected my discomfort. It seems strange now, but my only reply was to frantically scan the crowded foyer, hoping to spot Gigi.

"'Can I help you find someone?' offered the solicitous greeter, who told me that her name was Martha Davis. I asked her if she knew Gigi DeMarco.

"'Are you Gigi's co-worker? She instructed me to be on the lookout for you, but she didn't tell me you would be so beautiful. We better get some help finding you a seat. Wait here for just a moment.'

"Almost instantly, Martha returned with a distinguished gray-haired gentleman, whom she introduced humorously as, 'Our best usher and my better half, Frank Davis.' On the way into the sanctuary, Frank pointed out the restrooms, water fountain, and information table.

"Martha also gave me a church bulletin, which I clutched tightly. My other hand encircled the small navy purse that matched my suit. I didn't bother taking my Bible, because it would have been too hypocritical. Since my junior year

102

in college when I started seeing Jon Blevins, I hadn't even opened the Bible that my father had given me shortly before his death. I was too afraid to open it for fear the wrath of God would somehow jump off the once familiar pages. I assumed there would be pew Bibles and hymnals to follow along with during the service. Remember, this was before smartphones and tablets with electronic Bible apps, so many churchgoers brought their own Bibles.

"Anyhow, I panicked again when I realized Frank Davis was escorting me to the very front of the church. There, on the first row, was a seat with a paper with my name written in Gigi's familiar handwriting. On the left side of me sat Gigi's oldest daughter, Janet, who was holding her squirming newborn son, Joshua.

"I smiled at Janet, but I could barely look at Joshua, because whenever I saw a tiny infant, I felt a flood of guilt and grief. Quickly, I glanced to my right side and was greeted by the engaging smile and warm handshake offered to me by graduating seminarian John Martin."

Cassie stopped talking and covered her mouth in dismay. "Katie, I must be boring you to tears, telling you every detail of our first meeting. I'm sorry. I've never shared the complete story with anyone, and talking about it reminds me of what a miracle meeting my precious John really was."

"Don't you dare be sorry, darling girl. And don't you dare stop, either. You are finally getting to the good part, and I really do have all afternoon."

"Okay, Katie, if you insist. Because I was so self-conscious when I took my seat, I was unaware of the way the 24-year-old newly ordained minister was staring at me. When I did realize, I immediately thought something must be wrong with the way that I was dressed. After a quick mental checklist, I reassured myself that I had foreseen every detail of my appearance.

"I remember wondering, *Why is John Martin studying me like I have some secret that he is trying to uncover? Is he one of those prophetic pastors who can look through me and see the sin that has changed my life forever?*

"John instantly sensed my discomfort and whispered nonchalantly, 'Please forgive me for staring, but you remind me of someone.' John tried to regain his own composure since he was feeling anything but nonchalant. Months later, he told me that I looked exactly like the kind of woman he had always prayed would someday be his wife.

"When we met, John was 5'10" in height, and his weight was barely 170 pounds. He always believed his wife would be a tall, slim brunette. I guess I fit the bill at 5'7" and weighing about 130 pounds." Her cheeks flooded with a rosy color.

I laughed. "Cassie, those Pilates must really work, because you can't weigh a pound more now."

Cassie smiled at the compliment. "But John said it was my hazel eyes that intrigued him most. He told me he was first attracted to my eyes, which he thought were mesmerizing." She blushed again.

In a solemn tone she recalled, "Due to his sensitive nature, John also noticed a brokenness about me contradicting my confident appearance. When he attempted to calm my anxiety by reassuring me I merely reminded him of someone, he heard what he believed was God's still small voice saying, 'John, this woman is your future wife, but she has experienced great pain. It is your gentleness that will win her heart.'

"He wasn't accustomed to God speaking to him so directly, since the only other time he had heard a specific message was when he was called to ministry. After being a pastor for almost two decades, he has learned to better discern when God is speaking. But back then, he wondered if it really was God's voice. He teased me later that it might have only been wishful thinking on his own part, hoping I might be the answer to his prayers.

"John tried to keep himself calm by distractedly running his fingers through his crop of thick blond hair. This caused the cowlick at the part on his hairline to stand straight up. Now, it was my turn to stare. *Should I tell the minister his hair looked a fright?* I was worried, certain that he would be called to speak to the congregation. It seemed peculiar to me, because I found myself feeling protective of this unassuming young man.

"'Your hair is a bit tousled,' I said softly. However, the music had started at the very minute I had spoken. John seemed perplexed, so I pointed to his hair and then smoothed my own brunette mane in explanation. He looked at me quizzically again, but then seemed to understand my concern. Intuitively, he drew his right hand to the exact spot where I had pointed and tamed the stubborn cowlick.

"I smiled to acknowledge that John had taken care of

the problem. John smiled back in appreciation for my caring enough to be concerned about his appearance on this special day. He said he was thinking about a lot more.

"While we were exchanging this innocent smile, something supernatural was occurring within John. He thought back to the words of his grandmother, Lucy Martin, who had cautioned him to be open to the reality of true love – whenever and wherever – it showed up. 'Someday, you'll be smitten by a young woman, and she'll win your heart before you even know what's happening, Johnny,' Grandma Lucy had repeatedly proclaimed.

"Katie, I was totally unaware that anything was happening in John's heart, because my own heart was so numb and tattered. It had never recovered from being broken by my English professor."

Chapter 9
The Beginning of Forgiveness

EVEN THOUGH WE had been sitting at that old oak table in the kitchen of the parsonage for more than an hour, I wanted Cassie to finish telling me all about how she had fallen in love with her husband. I had probably bored her to tears, telling her every little detail of my time with my Jake. Now that he was gone, all I had were my memories.

In Cassie's case, there were a lot of new memories to be made, but some old ones had to be healed first. "Come on, sweetie. Tell me more about the morning you met Pastor John. You know I won't want to leave until I hear the whole story."

"Well, when I met John, I didn't notice whether he was particularly handsome, because I was captivated by his kindness and genuine concern for my well-being. John was just completing his theological coursework for a Master's degree in divinity at Manning University in New Jersey, but he was also filling in as an interim pastor for a small independent Bible church in Lima, Pennsylvania.

"I attended a nondenominational church while growing up, and truthfully I didn't know much about theology or denominations. All I knew was that when Pastor John Martin smiled at me, the hopelessness in my heart temporarily disappeared.

"I felt that same comfort when Gigi sang *Amazing Grace* that Sunday morning. The lyrics seemed to be perfect for my situation, 'Amazing Grace, how sweet the sound that saved a wretch like me.' Her classically trained voice was beautiful, but it was not her technique or talent, but rather God's anointing which made the song meaningful. The lyrics promised that grace was available even for someone as wretched as I had been.

"Then, when John stepped on the platform to deliver a brief sermon titled, 'The Amazing Ways of the Creator,' I found myself listening intently to this young Bible scholar who had no idea that his words were like a glass of cool water to my thirsty soul.

"Part of his sermon dealt with the power of forgiveness, explaining how we must not only be willing to forgive others, but that we also must forgive ourselves for the times when we have failed. *Is he reading my mind?* I wondered.

"Pastor John said that forgiveness is truly a divine gift, but that it is available to all. My broken heart was filled with optimism for the first time in years. *I could be forgiven?* There was still hope for me. Now, that was amazing.

"After the service, John stood next to the podium and was greeted by lots of well-wishers. I sat alone in my seat in the front row, unaware of his constantly watchful eye. I was sad because I was mindful that I would probably never see the youthful pastor again. The only reason I hadn't left sooner was because I was waiting for Gigi to finish talking to all the people who were complimenting her on her solo.

"Finally, Gigi was free. 'It was lovely, Gigi. Thank you for inviting me.'

"'You're coming to lunch, aren't you?' Gigi asked. 'We're having a gathering at my house to celebrate Pastor John's special day.'

"'Gigi, thank you, but I couldn't possibly intrude.' I wanted to say, 'Yes, I'll come,' since it would give me another chance to see John Martin, but that seemed ridiculous. I didn't think I was the kind of girl that a pastor would be interested in. I hadn't even had a date since I had ended my affair with Jon Blevins.

"'What do you mean, you're not coming?' Pastor John Martin frowned as he spoke these words from where he stood. I hadn't realized that he had overheard my conversation with Gigi. 'It would be such a disappointing day if I had a chance to meet you and then you mysteriously disappeared without having lunch. You must be starving, Cassie. I know I am.'

"I laughed, because I didn't realize that ministers could joke. From the first moment that I met John Martin, I felt both safe and wanted – two things I had never felt with Jon Blevins. 'Okay, I'll come for a sandwich,' I replied, 'but then I'll have to hurry back to my files at the museum.'

"John clapped his hands in delight, and I laughed again. I

had laughed more in the last hour than I had in months. John and I followed Gigi outside, where her husband was waiting.

"'I have my car here,' I said. 'I'll follow you to your house.'

"'Could you please give a starving preacher a ride?' John grinned playfully, and tried to sound casual.

"This request was out of character for the clergyman who prided himself on never being alone with a young woman, but I didn't know that then. From our first glance, John was convinced I was the 'girl' for him. At any rate, he detected it would be an uphill undertaking to persuade me of this, but love won out.

"Katie, the rest of the story is history. John and I have spent sixteen wonderful years together, although no marriage is perfect. Speaking of that, maybe you have some advice about what I wrote concerning our lack of intimacy. I appreciate that you didn't bring the subject up, waiting patiently until I was ready to talk about it. Despite our recent lack of physical closeness, my treasure of a husband is the kind of man I thought I had forfeited the chance to have. I am so grateful that God is a God of second chances."

"Since you've broached the topic, I do have a suggestion about someone who might be able to shed some light on your problem. Lizzie's granddaughter, Dr. Jasmine Jones, is a highly respected psychologist and family therapist affiliated with the Cleveland Clinic. I might have mentioned her to you before. Anyway, I hope you don't mind, but I contacted Jasmine to ask her if she deals with marital issues of a sexual nature, saying that I had some friends who might need a little help. She does, Cassie, and I promise you that you can trust her to be completely confidential. Plus, she's a devoted Christian believer, even though I assume she can't disclose this detail in the secular professional setting where she's employed. I've known Jazz since she was a little girl, and she takes after her late grandmother in the integrity of her character. Lizzie never shared my secrets, and you can trust that Jasmine won't share yours, either."

"Oh, I've been praying about finding someone to help us navigate through this, Katie. Dr. Jones sounds like a wonderful idea. Could I see her without John the first time, and would you be willing to come along? I could sure use some moral support. The only snag is that I'm not sure if our insurance will cover it."

"On Saturday mornings, Jasmine donates a few hours at a Christian counseling center in Cleveland. She's willing to see you there at no charge for an initial consultation, and the center has a sliding scale if insurance is a problem in the future. If it's okay with you, I'll call her to get an appointment for you. I'll be happy to go with you for support, but don't you think your husband should be the one to be there?"

"Yes, Katie, but I'd like to get acquainted with Dr. Jones before John comes along. You already know all my dreadful secrets, and would be a tremendous advocate on the initial visit."

"Everyone has secrets." I placed my hand over Cassie's hand that was resting on her golden oak kitchen table. Then I gave her hand a little squeeze for encouragement. "It's just more isolating for you, because you are the pastor's wife, and you have had to keep your secrets locked inside. I think that's what makes them seem so terrible, because you never had the opportunity to find freedom from your emotional pain. I'll be praying that Jasmine will be that first step to true healing."

"Oh, dear precious Katie, you have been that first step to healing. I have been so blessed by your friendship and confidence."

"Thanks, sweetie. Now, back to more of the story about you and Pastor John's courtship. It's not history to me, so I want to hear all the details."

Cassie stood and put the empty teacups in the kitchen sink. "It's just your typical run-of-the-mill romance novel. John swept me off my feet with cards, roses, and dinner out whenever he could afford to take me. Being a struggling young minister, his income was meager, so most often he bought me a single red rose because he couldn't afford a whole dozen. He would pick wildflowers for me, too, knowing how much I liked them.

"We became inseparable, spending time going to free concerts, lectures, and museums, because in a city like Philadelphia there are lots of activities that don't cost anything. Then, on Sunday mornings, I started attending church to support John while he was preaching. Soon, listening to his sermons, I began to understand fully about the amazing forgiveness that's available to us, no matter what we've done.

"Gigi started planning our wedding even before we were engaged. A few months after I met John's grandmother, Lucy

Martin, she gave him the beautiful diamond engagement ring that his late grandfather, Robert, had given her. As she aged, arthritis in her hands had kept her from being able to wear it."

Cassie lovingly looked at the round ¾-carat diamond solitaire set in platinum on her left hand. "'I want Cassie to have this when it's the right time, Johnny,' his grandmother had told him. 'It's written all over your face that she's the one. Remember when I told you that you would know? Well, I know too.'

"It was a couple of weeks later on Valentine's Day, when John took me to supper at our favorite place, Da Shin's Chinese Restaurant in Media, Pennsylvania. The little family-owned bistro was where we had our first date. John got down on one knee and proposed, ceremoniously offering his grandmother's ring to me. When he asked me to marry him, I was speechless. The restaurant staff and the patrons were all staring at us, waiting excitedly for my answer. You would think I would have been overcome with joy, but instead I was confused. It all happened so fast, and I hadn't had time to tell him any of my secrets."

Tears filled Cassie's eyes when she said, "I wanted to tell him about my father's suicide, my affair with Jon Blevins, and about miscarrying the baby, but every time an opportunity arose, I was too afraid of losing him.

"Almost from the beginning, sensing how serious we were I did tell John that I had an 'accident' in college, and the doctor said I would probably never be able to have children. I told him this, because I figured anyone who was going into ministry must love children, and he wouldn't want a wife who was unable to conceive a child."

"You tried to push him away, and it didn't work?" I asked. At the same time, I couldn't help but notice the blazing crimson maple trees in the parsonage's backyard as the window just behind Cassie framed them beautifully. I hoped someday she would paint the exquisite autumn scene.

"Perhaps, I did." Her mood grew even more somber. "But John's only reaction was to comfort me, remarking how he better understood my frequently downcast expression. He kissed me tenderly, reassuring me that a pastor has to care for so many people's children, he didn't need any of his own.

"A couple months later, John commented that adopting a child can be an excellent remedy for a childless couple, because there are countless kids without a good home. This happened after one of the families in the church flew to Korea to pick up a baby girl they adopted from there."

"Maybe he wanted to adopt. Anyway, don't you think your husband had a right to know the truth?"

"Well, Katie, I don't know about adopting. That's the only time he mentioned it. As for the truth, I wish I would have had the courage to tell him. But when he was down on one knee proposing, I was afraid that if I didn't say, 'Yes,' I might miss my chance at being with the most wonderful man I had ever met. After Grandma Lucy's ring was on my finger, almost immediately plans for our wedding were in full swing. His family was excited, and so was mine, I just couldn't tell him for fear my dream would be shattered."

"Is there something else you aren't sharing? My maternal instincts are leading me to presume you're withholding a crucial detail."

"It might sound as if I'm only defending myself, but once I did tell John there was some personal history he should be aware of before we married. His reply was rather strange. 'Everyone has a few skeletons, and there are things best left between an individual and God.'

"John passionately declared there was absolutely nothing I could say that would cause him to not want to marry me. His exact words were, 'Silly girl, don't you know I'm head over heels, hopelessly, and helplessly in love with you?'

"We had a beautiful June wedding. I admit I felt like an imposter in my full-length white lace gown with seed pearl and sequin accents, but it had been my mother's. My sheer veil fell from a glittering rhinestone tiara. Because my father was gone, my paternal grandfather gave me away. Here are a few photos I got out, because I knew you would enjoy seeing them."

"Oh, my. What an exquisite bride! You were a vision, and Pastor John has so much hair. You both look like kids."

"Yes, we were young and so much in love," Cassie said almost giggling. "Here's a picture of Grandpa Kirk walking me down the aisle. He looked so proud dressed in his tuxedo filling in for the son he had never stopped blaming himself for losing to suicide. I wasn't worried anyone would ever tell John about the circumstances of my father's death, because my family never spoke of it. As for the affair with Jon Blevins and the baby, no one, not even my mother, suspected anything about it."

"Wouldn't you feel better if Pastor John knew about all this?"

"Of course, I would. But, let me explain another disappointing reality that you must hold in confidence."

I nodded reassuringly.

"John and I rarely talk about anything personal. We never seemed to connect that way. Don't get me wrong, we adore each other. But for some reason, there is a wall that keeps us from sharing our hearts with each other."

"Honey, secrets have a way of causing that wall to go up. Before you can talk about anything else, you might have to tell that husband of yours the truth. I'm a lot older than you, and my Jake taught me a lot about loving a man. Men can sense when you are hiding something, and they are afraid it might have something to do with them. Your past has nothing to do with Pastor John. It's just my opinion, but it seems he has a right to know the circumstances that wounded you so deeply."

"After all these years?" Cassie sounded almost desperate.

But I held my ground. "Again, it's only my opinion, and I'm not a psychologist, but Dr. Jasmine Jones is. Maybe this has something to do with the intimacy problems you are experiencing. I'll make that appointment right away, and you can ask her for her professional advice about what to do with all these secrets."

I stood up and looked at my watch. "No time like the

present, sweet girl. Jasmine said she would make fitting you in a priority. I don't think you give your man enough credit though. Well, I have to get back to the coffee shop and help Brianna get it closed up for the day. She's really been doing a great job on her own lately, but closing up alone is something she's not quite ready for."

Cassie escorted me to the front porch. Then as I was leaving, her neighbor called out to her. "Do you have time for a cup of coffee, Cassie? I heard something that you and Pastor John should know about."

I saw Cassie's distressed look and intervened. "Pauline, why don't you come down to my shop and have a cup of coffee? I've been meaning to ask you how to bake that fabulous apple pie you're famous for. I would like to add it to our menu. Cassie's had a taxing afternoon, and she needs to get supper on before Pastor John gets home. He's been so busy, she hasn't had a chance to spend time with him for the past couple days." Cassie shot me a look of thankfulness, and seemed relieved that she would be spared of trying to deal with her sometimes gossipy neighbor lady.

Pauline was thrilled that I wanted her expert advice, because she loved being an expert about anything. "Of course, I'll come to the coffee shop right now," she said proudly. "I'll get a chance to chat with Cassie later."

In her heart, the pastor's wife sensed that Katie was right. She had always believed that John should know the truth about why she was so merciful to those who fell from grace.

Surprisingly, Cassie's compassion even extended to Jon

Blevins now. Two decades earlier, she had eagerly embraced the bitterness produced by her professor's betrayal. Then at the beginning of her marriage, after months of digesting her husband's sermons about forgiveness, she finally embraced the divine gift for herself. Yet initially it horrified the young bride to contemplate God's expectation for her to also forgive her former lover.

After much soul-searching, Cassie ultimately relinquished bitterness, replacing it with genuine prayer, not wanting to be imprisoned by hostility and hatred. She didn't think of Jon Blevins often, as so much time had passed. When she did, Cassie would pray for him to find an authentic relationship with the Savior who died for both of their sins.

As a minister's wife, she had observed enough men and women like Blevins – endeavoring to fill the empty hole in their heart created only for Jesus with some addictive behavior. For her married instructor, it wasn't alcohol and drugs, materialism, or even work, it was with women who didn't belong to him.

Cassie empathized with anyone emotionally tormented or spiritually bankrupt, because she was once a woman in desperate need of grace herself. That grace had come in the form of John Martin's steadfast love.

Chapter 10
The Keeper of All Secrets

FOR SOME REASON, Cassie decided to follow my advice and tell her husband all about everything that very night. It wasn't something she planned. I have to admit I was surprised that she didn't wait to talk with Jasmine first, but I guess the Holy Spirit nudged her into finally telling the truth.

My spiritual daughter wrote about it in one of her stories — those narratives where she writes about herself as if she were someone else. No one else will probably ever see it, but I am sure glad she trusted me with what happened. This time the details are all there, except for the part where the poor child hardly got any sleep at all that night. Instead she got out of bed and sat at her desk for a couple of hours penning this account.

Late that evening, when her husband returned from visiting his church member at the Cleveland Clinic, Cassie whipped up a shepherd's pie for him. The Irish casserole was one of John's favorites, and they always laughed about the significance of the name.

When John began eating, his custom was to bury himself in his thoughts and the task of spooning the delicious dish into his mouth. Their standard topics of conversation were normally the church, Cassie's artwork, or some practical matter like paying bills or a repair that the parsonage needed.

Pastor John didn't realize how exceptionally quiet his wife was being that evening. After an exhausting day, John's sense of discernment was at an all-time low. That's why it took him by surprise when he got up from the table and began to head for his office to study, when Cassie almost cried out, "John, we need to talk."

"Oh, I'm sorry, honey, please forgive me. I didn't realize something was troubling you. You sound like it's serious. Is it your mother?" Cassie's mom had been experiencing some heart problems recently.

She quickly shook her head and said, "No."

"Is someone in the congregation ill?" The minister was overwhelmed by his workload, because the church couldn't afford a full-time associate. Part-time associate, Pastor Ginger Graham was swamped overseeing the small group, recovery, and discipleship programs. The seniors' pastor, Ron Jacobs, a 75-year-old retired missionary, assisted with visitation. Having five decades of ministry service, Rev. Jacobs was an ally to his lead pastor, but health issues limited his working hours considerably. Regardless, hospitalized churchgoers can get offended when John Martin doesn't visit them personally. It's an impossible task with so many aging members. Therefore, John is often distracted, but seldom insensitive, and Cassie's visible distress was alarming him.

"No one's ill, John. There are a few things I should have told you years ago. I hadn't planned on telling you any of this tonight, but I can't keep it inside any longer. This afternoon while I was speaking with Katie, it's like an emotional dam burst, and I seem to be at a dangerous flood level. I was going to talk to the psychologist first, and then..."

"Psychologist? Cassie, I have no idea what you are talking about, and you are really beginning to frighten me."

"Could we please sit down in the living room and turn the fireplace on to take the chill off the house? We can have coffee while we talk."

Now, John Martin was perplexed. This was out of character for the woman he loved. He knew Cassie tried diligently not to burden him with unnecessary problems when he had had a demanding day. She was the perfect pastor's wife, anticipating his needs and the needs of many in their church. He couldn't imagine what was happening that was causing her to act so distressed. Looking closely at her for the first time that evening, he also realized her eyes were red and swollen as if she had been crying.

The couple sat down on their burgundy leather sofa together, the sofa Cassie's mother had given to them when she'd bought a new couch. Cassie took a deep breath, then almost timidly began to speak. "John, I know that I shoulder much of the blame for why we don't communicate better. It's difficult to talk about intimate issues when one partner keeps secrets from the other, and I have kept secrets from you our entire married life."

Pastor John Martin couldn't believe what he was hearing. He prided himself on being a good listener. He'd even taken several pastoral counseling courses when he studied for the ministry. Often, he was the person his parishioners would choose to confess some dark issue that they had hidden from those they loved. Besides, this was his wife of more than 15 years; if he knew anyone, he thought he knew his Cassie. His world seemed to be crumbling around him. He braced himself for whatever the woman he loved was about to tell him.

Cassie's hazel eyes turned the intense shade of green they always did whenever she was upset. In the fire's glow, the auburn highlights in her hair shone, and she looked so vulnerable and alone that John decided, whatever Cassie revealed, he would extend God's mercy to her.

"John, there's no easy way to tell you any of this. So, let me begin by confessing that I am not as successful at my artwork as I have led you to believe. My paintings don't sell very frequently, and I never wanted to burden you by asking you for more money from our already tight budget. About a decade ago, I began selling small antique and vintage collectibles online and at consignment stores...."

John laughed in relief, interrupting Cassie, who suddenly was the one confused by his unexpected reaction. Seeing her concern, John quickly said, "Honey, I have known about your little hobby almost from the beginning. Truthfully, it reminded me of the industrious woman we read about in Proverbs 31 who takes care of her family through her resourcefulness."

"Why didn't you ever tell me that you knew, John?"

"It broke my heart that your paintings didn't sell very often. I could see how discouraged you were, yet how much pleasure you derived from your artwork. I noticed the antique dishes and jewelry you were endlessly organizing. Besides, when the statements came from the galleries for tax purposes, there wasn't a lot of revenue. I hesitated approaching the subject, anxious you might stop painting."

"How considerate of you, John. Thank you for allowing me the dignity of letting me believe you thought of me as an accomplished artist."

"Sweetheart, you are successful in God's eyes. You create beauty with your paintings, and you have a servant's heart when it comes to using your artistic gifting for God's kingdom. What about the murals you paint in the children's classrooms wherever we go? I don't measure success in monetary terms, and you shouldn't either. Our Heavenly Father never does. Now that your little secret is out...."

"No, John, there's a lot more." The pastor's wife was the one interrupting this time. "I never told you the entire truth about my father's death."

"The truth?" John asked quizzically. "I know your father was seriously ill for quite a few years, and then he died the week before your 14th birthday. This was a terrible heartbreak for you. I can see it in your eyes almost every time you mention your dad."

"Those details are true, but they're only part of the story." Cassie took a sip of coffee from her mug. Stalling for time, she ran her finger around the rim of her cup. Then she took a deep breath and finally continued in a voice that was barely audible. "My father suffered from chronic depression coupled with what we realized after his death was a serious addiction issue. He did not die from natural causes."

John's eyes seemed to grow quite wide and fill with confusion as he repeated in a questioning tone, "Natural causes?"

"My father took his life by shooting himself with his own gun. Early one morning, my mother found him slumped over the wheel of his pickup truck in our garage. Her blood-curdling scream awakened me. When I ran into the garage, I saw my dad, the man I loved more than my own life, bleeding profusely from a gunshot wound to the head. My mother told me to call 911, but it was too late." Cassie began to sob loudly, as if her father's suicide had just happened.

"Honey, I had no idea. I am terribly sorry." John reached for his distraught spouse and pulled her to him. He encircled her tightly within his strong arms, whispering, "It's going to be all right, baby. I wish you would have told me sooner. I could have been here to listen and to pray for you."

It was his turn to breathe a sigh of relief. This was Cassie's deep, dark secret. He wondered why she hadn't told him this before. "Did you think I wouldn't understand? Or that it would reflect poorly on your father?"

Cassie gently pulled away from him. "I'm not sure why I didn't tell you, John. It was as if my family shared a pact not to reveal the truth about what happened. I guess you would call it a lie of omission." She brushed her tears away with both of her hands, then blew her nose on a tissue that she found in the pocket of her hand-knitted sweater. Delores Hall, a beloved mentor and the wife of their former district superintendent, had knitted the beautiful ivory cardigan especially for her. Cassie wore it whenever she felt insecure and in need of special grace. If she ever needed the reassurance of God's presence, today was the day.

Cassie hadn't changed her clothes since meeting with Katie earlier. Being reminded of Katherine Montague, she knew that the next time she visited the coffee shop Katie would want to know how Pastor John reacted to the disclosure about her past. Maybe because she knew that Katie was already praying or simply because she could not keep her secrets buried inside of her for another day, Cassie blurted out, "There's more."

There's more? Pastor John Martin wanted to get up and run out the front door of the parsonage before his wife could say anything else. The woman he thought he knew completely was suddenly a stranger to him. Cassie looked as though she was about to become violently ill. Her husband sensed that there was no stopping whatever was going to come next, so he emotionally braced himself.

"Do you remember when we were dating, and I told you that I would probably never be able to have children?"

"Of course, sweetheart. That was a huge confidence to share so early in our courtship. Although I felt like you were trying to drive me away when you told me."

"Maybe I was, John. I never wanted to have to tell you the whole truth. You had a right to know, but I was doubtful you would want to marry me, if you were aware of what I had done."

It was all her husband could do to not react. He didn't even move a facial muscle, uneasy Cassie might perceive any response as judgment. Engulfed by God's peace, the seasoned minister within him took over. From his pastoral training, he knew whatever was haunting his mate had to come out. "Go ahead, Cassie. Tell me what's been tormenting you all these years," he urged. Pastor John had counseled enough folks to grasp the power of hidden hurts or sin in holding people captive. They become spiritually whole by releasing and exposing their often shame-filled secrets to the light of God's love.

"John, I didn't lie and pretend I was a virgin while we were dating. Yet you were incredibly honorable during those months before our wedding, never pressuring me for sex. You really lived what you believed. You never pushed for more information, but I should have told you that when I was in college…." Cassie stopped abruptly. She was terrified to continue, fearing what her words would do to her spouse.

Long ago, John Martin remembered explaining to his

then future wife that everyone has a few skeletons. The truth was, he hadn't wanted to share any of his. Now that he could see the toll that holding things inside had caused her, he wanted her to let go of whatever it was. As a minister, he had witnessed firsthand over and over the desire most human beings have to confess their sin and to be forgiven.

"Whatever it is, get it out. We can deal with it together." His professional detachment and unusual calmness were giving John Martin the courage to hear what his wife had to say.

Cassie hung her head like a child who had been bad. She didn't look up as she started speaking again. "In college, I became involved with one of my instructors. I had an affair with a man named Dr. Jon Blevins that lasted for about a year." When she glanced up to see her husband's reaction, there were no tears in her eyes. Instead, Cassie Martin seemed to have been transported to another time, completely lost in the memories of her past.

John thought that his spouse must have chosen the wrong word to describe her relationship with her professor. He had never told her, but he knew she wasn't a virgin when they married. He had always been good at reading people, and her obvious guilt had been a dead giveaway. "An affair?"

Now that she had started, there was no turning back. "My professor was married, and he had a couple of small children. It all started innocently. He wanted my advice on a novel he was writing. I was flattered by his attention, not realizing

127

that he was a ladies' man who used his charm on naïve coeds like me."

She took a deep breath, and since her husband had no reaction, she continued. "I was just one among the many, but I didn't know that until after it ended badly."

I can handle this. A young, innocent college student is seduced by an older, worldly professor. It happens all the time, and has nothing to do with me. Pastor John Martin was feeling compassionate, relieved, and ready to comfort his wife, who appeared to be agonizing over her past mistake. "Honey, I know firsthand how poor choices can cause an individual great pain, but like I always preach on Sundays, 'The same forgiveness you extend to others, you must extend to yourself.'"

For the first time since they had started this conversation, Cassandra Martin smiled tentatively. "John, you were the one who taught me about forgiveness. I didn't know anything about it until I met you. You are such a good preacher. When we were dating, after listening to your sermons for a few months, I began to understand God's forgiveness. I've just never been sure if you could forgive me."

Again, he reached out to embrace her, but her body felt rigid in his arms. *Please, don't tell me there's another secret,* he thought. But, the wise pastor bravely said, "Is there something you aren't telling me?"

This time Cassie pulled away from her caring spouse almost violently. Her eyes seemed as wild as a wounded animal. "I discovered I was pregnant with Jon Blevins' child shortly before catching my first glimpse of him with his wife and children. For a year, he had insisted he didn't love her and she didn't love him. When I saw the look of adoration in her eyes, I knew he had been lying to me. Worse, she was pregnant too, a fact that he had conveniently forgot to mention."

The confused clergyman hadn't heard anything beyond "pregnant with Jon Blevins' child." He couldn't think. His head was swimming and he desperately needed some fresh air. *I have to get out of here.*

A few parishioners had confided in him about experiencing panic attacks. He had never identified with their inability to be rational and cope with a stressful situation. He was always a man in control. Not now, though. His heart was beating out of his chest, and he couldn't breathe or bear to hear one more word from a woman he once thought he knew as well as he knew himself. Apparently, he didn't know his wife at all. The panic-stricken minister jumped up off of the sofa, bolting for the front door. Then he opened it and ran down the porch steps onto the darkened street without a destination in mind.

"John! Please, talk to me, John! Don't leave right now. John....!" Cassie called after him, too frightened to move from the couch.

As he slammed the front door shut, his wife's voice sounded muffled and far away. He didn't try to make out her words. He had to get away. *A child!* Cassie had been pregnant with another man's child. She had lied to him. Pastor John Martin had a secret too. He had never told Cassie how desperately he had wanted children of his own. He had given up the desire to be a father in exchange for the opportunity to spend his life with her.

"Pastor John! Pastor Martin!" Pauline Alana called out to him shrilly as he hurried past her house. John Martin was not stopping for anyone. "Please, Pastor John, I have something that you and Cassie need to know."

Hearing the word, "Please," the compassionate man instinctively stopped in his tracks. But when Pauline saw his distraught grimace – illuminated by the glow from her porch light – she said sheepishly, "I'm sorry. It looks like it might not be a good time," and quickly ducked back inside her house.

Providentially, the hurting pastor suddenly knew where he needed to go. All John Martin could think about was that he had to get inside of his church, which was next to the parsonage. He slipped into a neighbor's yard heading for the stone-covered alley that would take him back to his destination without anyone seeing him. His hands were shaking so badly that he fumbled with his keys as he unlocked the sanctuary door. He walked to the empty altar and knelt rocking back and forth on the carpeted floor while crying out loud, "Why God? Why?" Uncustomary tears were streaming from the middle-aged preacher's eyes, and he buried his face in his hands.

Cassandra Martin sat immobile on the leather couch. She hadn't moved since John had dashed out the front door. *I knew things would never be the same if I told him my secrets. John can't possibly love me after all he knows. Why did I tell him? Why?* The questions in her mind trailed off as fatigue set in.

The pastor's wife cried until she couldn't cry any more. Then she got up from the sofa, put their coffee mugs in the sink, turned off the lights, and headed for the bedroom. For the first time in her married life, she let the dirty supper dishes sit on the table. She felt too dirty herself to clean anything up.

She didn't know where John was, and she was worried about him, but she had to lie down. She was exhausted from the events of the day, and she had already resigned herself to the fact that he could never forgive her.

As the hours passed, Pastor John Martin was grappling with his own dark night of the soul. He knew that no matter what, he should forgive. It was what he had always taught others. But if he did forgive his wife, how could he ever trust her again?

The logical part of John's personality that ministered to lots of other folks when they were in conflict reminded him that he didn't know the whole story. Where was the child? Had there ever been a child? Had his wife had an abortion and hidden that from him too? Why couldn't Cassie have children? She had never fully explained that. It must have been a fact, since despite never taking any precautions, they had never conceived.

It was chilly and unusually dark at almost 6 a.m., when the emotionally depleted preacher quietly tiptoed into the bedroom he shared with a woman who now seemed like a total stranger. As he watched Cassie sleeping fitfully, he admitted that he hadn't known her at all...not the fragmented, broken parts that made her who she was. Still, with the moonlight streaming in the window and falling on her face, she was as beautiful as the day they had met.

During the long hours of that night at the altar of the Maple Avenue Community Church, the minister had struggled with his mate's betrayal. Cassie had been a lost sheep before she'd known him, and God had used his love to heal her. If he was honest, he had always realized she had secrets.

In the beginning, he had been afraid to ask her, for fear whatever it was would frighten her away. Later, he'd been too tired and consumed with church business, and she'd seemed to be okay. He had been just as guilty as she was for letting a wall go up between them. After all, he had secrets too. He was convinced after all his years in ministry that most people had things in their past that caused them shame, even though few would admit it.

"John, is that you?" Cassie's voice was timid. "Please, forgive me, I never meant to hurt you."

"Cassie, there's something I have to ask you." With resignation, the weary pastor sat down on the bed next to where she was lying and turned on the brass bedside lamp. "What happened to your child? I need to know."

"Are you sure you want to hear more now? You've been up all night, and I've never seen you look so exhausted." His blondish-gray hair was tousled, his blue eyes were bloodshot and puffy, and the lines in his brow seemed deeper. Cassie felt guilty that her deception had caused her husband to experience such heartbreak.

"When I counsel other folks, I always tell them, 'Sometimes, it has to get worse before it can get better.' I want to hear it all now and get it over with." Then he sighed heavily.

Cassie heard his sigh, but she also heard him offer her a glimmer of hope when he said, "...before it gets better." *Could it possibly get better?*

"You're sure that this is the time?" Cassie asked.

Pastor John was too tired to speak. He just nodded emphatically.

"There was never a child," she lamented in a sorrowful voice. She wanted to reach for her husband's hand, but the fear of rejection stopped her. More out of obedience than courage, she reluctantly described the accident resulting in the loss of her baby. John Martin kept silent while Cassie filled in all the details.

"I never told anyone, John. Then, for some reason, I told Katie. She's been like a mother to me here in Maple Grove. In many ways, it's easier for me to talk to Katie than to my own mother. As I explained earlier, I guess my family quit telling the truth after my father died. It was just too painful to bear."

Cassie sat up in bed and pulled the covers around her, feeling autumn's cold chill through her silk nightgown. "Katie wondered if sharing my secrets with you would draw us closer, and besides I couldn't bear the guilt of deceiving you any longer. Again, I'm so sorry for hurting you and betraying your trust. I don't expect that you can ever forgive me."

"No, Cassie." John Martin paused. The pastor's wife braced herself for what she thought would surely follow, his confirmation that he could never forgive her tarnished past. Instead, when he spoke, the weary minister tenderly inquired, "Can you forgive me?"

Cassie was astonished. "For what, John?"

"First of all, dear wife, like all of God's children, I am a sinner in need of His grace. I've had my own sinful skeletons that I've never even contemplated sharing. Yet, I momentarily judged you for yours."

John's words confused Cassie. *"Sinful skeletons?"* Surely, John's past held no comparison to hers; although she was not about to interrupt her husband to find out. Desperately wanting to hear what he would say next, she pushed the question away.

The remorse in his voice was palpable. "In the past two decades, I have supported thousands of brokenhearted people, but my own faithful companion has been all alone suffering in silence. Can you forgive me for failing you as a husband?"

Cassie didn't think she had any tears left to cry, but instantly tears of joy streamed down her cheeks. "You still love me?" Her tone was childlike and filled with disbelief.

"Love you?" John reached for Cassie's left hand and then almost ceremonially kissed the wedding ring on her finger. "Cassie, you are the greatest gift God ever gave me. Please forgive me too, for bolting from the house without giving you a chance to explain about your miscarriage. I have to tell you that it was really rough for me when we were dating and

I found out that we would probably never have children. I wasn't truthful with you, since I told you that it didn't matter."

John was holding his wife in his arms now, smoothing her dark brown hair back from her face. "You wanted children?" Cassie instantly recognized how adeptly her spouse had hidden this important fact from her.

"I did, sweetheart, but I wanted you no matter what I had to give up, and I still do."

"Oh, John," she cried, as tears of gratitude streamed down her cheeks. "I never stopped grieving over my infertility. I was too scared to reveal my desire for children, fearing I would have to disclose my past. Having you love me seemed more than I deserved. Whatever your own long-ago mistakes might be, you are God's best, my knight in shining armor. I only wish you would have felt safe in sharing your battles with me."

"There is something else I need to tell you that I should have told you a few years ago. The pressure of ministry got the best of me at our last church, and I experienced my first case of genuine burnout. I had heard other clergy discuss it, but I had no idea it could be so debilitating and exhausting. I'm sorry that I hid it from you trying to resolve some issues myself."

"What issues, John?"

"Things like how to forgive people for putting so many expectations on me to solve their problems or how to control my schedule and not work all the time, and the list goes on and on. We both need to sleep, honey. For now, I simply want you to know that it's not your fault we haven't been making love very often. I have been battling with depression as a result of the burnout, and a doctor prescribed medication to keep the symptoms at bay. Unfortunately, the medicine also seems to keep me from experiencing any physical desire."

"Why didn't you tell me? I could have at least listened."

"I'm not sure why. Somehow, it made me feel like less of a man that I couldn't seem to handle the day-to-day pressures of life. Besides, like you said we haven't communicated very well in the past. Hopefully, that's going to change in the future."

"Sweet boy, I would like that more than anything in the world. We might have to have a little assistance in breaking free of these unhealthy communication patterns though. Would you be willing to see a family psychologist with me who is a special friend of Katie's? Her name is Dr. Jasmine Jones. She can see us at a clinic in Cleveland that provides services on a sliding scale, and Katie says she is absolutely confidential and a devout believer. I'll bet she will have dealt with other clergy families experiencing burnout from stress, as well."

"I always recommend outside Christian counseling to others when their problems are more complicated than I can deal with through pastoral counseling. I don't like to admit it, but I have to agree, we could use some advice that enables us to learn how to love each other better for the next forty years." John kissed Cassie's forehead, and then he said very seriously, "I don't want there to be any more secrets between us. I also want to make our relationship my top priority, rather than my position as the pastor. Of course, God has to be in first place – but you should be right under Him – not at the bottom of my list. Forgive me for that, also."

"Oh, precious husband, I am also so thankful to God for putting us together, and I know now that He has a wonderful plan to work everything out. I have always understood your pastor's heart about His people coming first, but thank you for saying you want me to be at the top of the list." Cassie repeated the words Katie told her Jake for over four decades, "You are the love of my life, John Martin."

"You are the love of my life, Cassie Martin." John echoed back, reaching over and turning the bedside lamp off. As the sun was rising, the pastor's wife snuggled close to her husband. Then he began to passionately kiss the only woman he had ever loved. In the past year, the only other time he kissed her like this was just that once on the night of the concert. This time, he wasn't going to stop. As he did, Cassie silently thanked her Heavenly Father, the Keeper of all secrets, for this second chance at love.

My eyes filled with tears as I finished reading Cassie's story about the night she was set free from her past. Never having had children, I had often wondered what it felt like to be a mother and to love your child and to feel that their victory was your own. I know now, because Cassie is free, and God used me in some small way to help her find His grace.

Glancing around my cozy little kitchen in the apartment

that had once been home to Doc Blackstone, I contemplate how much we have in common. Doc never had children either, but he sure delivered a lot of babies. He must have sat here with his morning cup of coffee reading the Bible and saying a prayer that he would know how to tend to all the sick folks that he would encounter that day. That's how I start my morning, reading a devotional and praying for wisdom and a divine appointment to encourage another hurting soul along the way.

As for Cassie, I guess she won't need me to go with her on that appointment to see Jasmine, and I'm so glad. Pastor John will be at her side.

Well, I better get to work. It's going to be another busy day at Katie's Coffee Corner, because you just never know who will be walking in the door.

The End for Now

*Always remember our Heavenly Father
is the Keeper of Secrets
Healing our pain and shame from the past with
His grace and forgiveness*

Book Club or Bible Study Discussion Questions

Secrets of the Pastor's Wife

While answering the following questions, if being used for a Bible Study group, whenever possible use Scripture as the basis for your answer by finding specific verses that support your opinion.

1) *Secrets of the Pastor's Wife* is largely based on the never-shared past mistakes and hidden tragedy of main character, Cassandra Martin. Do you believe that most women and men have secrets from their past that they hide? If so, why?

2) Cassie Martin has moved frequently due to her husband's career as a pastor. The couple has never owned a home, and although she tries to be grateful, she is obviously tired of living in a parsonage. Have you ever known a pastor's wife who has lived in housing provided by the church? Have you ever

wondered what her feelings about not having her own home might be like?

3) Have you ever had a neighbor, like Pauline Alana, who likes to gossip? As a believer, how did you deal with the situation?

4) Elizabeth "Lizzie" Jones is a very important character in regard to the narrator Katherine (Calloway) Montague's upbringing and ultimate life choices. As you were reading, were you aware of the significance of Lizzie's colorblind love for the Calloway family in the face of the racially charged tensions of the 1960s?

5) Katie Montague and her late husband, Jacob, appear to be the perfect couple. Yet there was a time early in their marriage when they separated. What did you think about Lizzie's advice to Katie that she should go home, and of her statement "inside of every man there's this little boy who needs the woman he loves to stay by his side"?

6) When Jake Montague dies, Katie decides to open a coffee shop at this new stage in her life. Did you find this plan believable? Why or why not? Without Katie's Coffee Corner would Katie and the pastor's wife ever have become close?

7) Young Cassie was disgusted when her high school boyfriend, Tim, dumped her for another girl, Tammy Bart, who had a history of being promiscuous. As a pre-teen, Tammy had been a victim of sexual abuse by her stepfather. Research indicates that there is sometimes a correlation between sexual violation and promiscuity. Why would this occur?

8) Why did Cassie Martin hide the fact that her father had died by suicide? How do you think this first secret ultimately affected her?

9) Were you shocked by the relationship between Cassie and Professor Jon Blevins? How did she become trapped in such unwholesome circumstances? What did you feel for or about her during this time?

10) When Cassie and Pastor John Martin first met, did you think that they were an evenly matched couple? Or did this pairing surprise you?

11) Why was Cassie never willing to share her secrets with Pastor John before they married? Did he have a right to know?

12) Have you ever heard the term, "Secrets make you sick?" Do you believe that this is true? If so, then how can someone be emotionally healed?

13) Is there any difference between a lie of omission and a lie of commission? How does any type of lie spiritually affect an individual and those who are in relationship with them?

14) One of the most important concepts in this book is that of forgiveness in relation to Cassie's forgiving herself, and then ultimately accepting her husband's forgiveness for withholding her secrets from him. How does the Biblical view of forgiveness differ from the secular viewpoint? Please use Scripture to explain this pivotal issue.

15) Why is it easier to forgive other people than it is to forgive ourselves? After all, Cassie Martin seemed to extend mercy and grace to everyone except herself.

16) Katie Montague turned out to be a worthy confidant, one who kept the secrets of the pastor's wife. Have you ever shared your own secrets with someone who was not trustworthy? How did that make you feel?

17) Did this short novel leave you wondering if Pastor John Martin should disclose some of his own "sinful skeletons" from the past? Would it help their marriage, if Cassie more fully understood her husband's life history?

18) Since in the end we realize that both Cassie and John wanted children, despite the fact they are now in their early forties, should they pursue this avenue? If so, through what method: fertility treatment, adoption, or fostering, etc.?

19) Why did Pastor John hide his struggle with ministry burnout and depression from his wife? How did this affect their relationship and intimacy?

20) What is your greatest takeaway from this book in terms of the importance of emotional healing concerning spiritual well-being? Will this be a catalyst for some kind of change in your own life, such as telling some of your own secrets to a trustworthy confidant or counselor?

Bonus Short Story

Not Just Another Casserole Lady
By Christina Ryan Claypool

Trish Delaney didn't know what a Casserole Lady was. It confused her when her best friend, Eve Hughes, accused her of acting like one.

"You're being ridiculous, Trish. Gary Brown's wife died only six months ago, and here you are marching over to his house with your Chicken Alfredo Lasagna. Let's face it; you didn't even use a disposable pan. That kind of says it all." Eve yawned and looked down at her chipped nails which Trish was busy filing.

Trish's emery board stopped mid-stroke. "It's been almost a year since Pam Brown died, but that's not the point. I don't understand what you're accusing me of, Eve. What's a Casserole Lady?"

"Seriously! You don't know about the Casserole Ladies?" Eve stared into her manicurist's bewildered brown eyes. She had forgotten how sheltered her friend's life had been.

Trish's gorgeous good looks defied her true innocence, since she was a dark-haired beauty. Her almost flawless complexion was still nearly wrinkle-free, despite the fact that she turned 49 on her last birthday.

But it is her Barbie doll figure that caused all the trouble. Over the years, the salon owner has exercised and watched her diet to keep in shape. She still wears a size 4. The same size she wore on her wedding day three decades ago.

Her husband, Bill, had been so proud of the girl he married. They'd met in high school when Trish was a sophomore. She played the clarinet in the Pep Band for the Meadow Springs basketball games when Bill was the star shooting guard.

It really was love at first sight for both of them. Although Trish was afraid that Bill was one of those conceited jocks who collected girlfriends for a hobby. It wasn't long before she found out that her "Billy" was a sweet farm boy at heart who hoped to one day become a veterinarian.

The two had married a few months after graduation, against both their parents' wishes. Trish had studied to become a hair stylist, supporting Bill as he pursued his dream of becoming a vet. During the long years of his schooling, she'd worked hard to make ends meet, never complaining about all the things they couldn't have.

"Look, Trish, I'm genuinely sorry. I sometimes forget you've lived the love story that most of us have only read about in romance novels." Eve's heart broke for the pain Trish had experienced losing her husband. "I know Bill is the only man you've ever loved, but he's gone now. You've got to learn to protect yourself. It's kind of a crazy world out there."

Trish didn't want Eve to talk about Bill's death. It had been two years since the car accident, but she hadn't even given his clothes to her church's thrift store yet. She meant to, but every time she began going through his belongings, she would start sobbing and put everything back.

Trying to distract Eve from this conversation, Trish held up a couple bottles of nail polish for her to choose from, knowing she would select the vivid shade of purplish red she always wore.

"*Fuchsia on Fire,* silly girl. You know I never want you to paint my nails with anything else." Thirty-five-year-old Eve had been Trish's customer for almost two decades.

When Trish first opened Style by Design, everyone who was anyone in Meadow Springs had to try it out. After all, by then Bill was a veterinarian practicing on the edge of town. Local ladies thought it prestigious to have their hair done by a doctor's wife, even if Dr. Delaney tended animals instead of people.

The Delaneys had invested a lot of hard-earned cash to make Style by Design resemble a cosmopolitan studio. The salon walls were painted pale pink, accented with a mural of flowering cherry blossom trees. Chandeliers with crystal prisms hung from the high ceiling, reflecting light everywhere, and freshly brewed coffee with a plate of homemade chocolates always tempted the clientele. Four other stylists now rented booths there, too.

When Trish and Eve first met, Eve was a high school junior wanting to look her best for prom. She loved the up-do complete with rhinestone accents that the hairdresser created for her. More than that, despite their age differences, Eve sensed that Trish would be her friend for life. And that's exactly what she had become.

At this moment, Eve decided she had better warn her best buddy about keeping her emotions in check. "Trish, I know you miss Bill like crazy, but he's gone now. You have to use a little wisdom, or you really will turn into a Casserole Lady."

"Will you please just spit it out, Eve? I told you I don't have any idea what a Casserole Lady is." While she spoke, the experienced manicurist carefully painted her friend's nails. Trish was used to talking while she worked, but she had to admit she was starting to get agitated.

"The definition of a Casserole Lady? OK, you know those retirement communities where the women outnumber the men?"

"Not really, Eve." Trish put the top back on the nail polish bottle.

"Well, that's not the point anyway. The point is when women are alone and getting older, they are often looking for a good man. And really, you can't blame them. It's hard for them to find a good catch, because usually men die before their wives. So when an older man is widowed, like my dad was last year when we lost my mother, these desperate females seem to come out of the woodwork offering sympathy, support, and of course, a casserole."

"A casserole?" Trish asked, not understanding what a casserole had to do with anything.

"Often the first plan of attack for these aggressive ladies is to stop by the grieving widower's home with a warm casserole. They know that the way to a man's heart really is through his stomach. My father was vulnerable when Mom died. I'm glad we were there to fend them off for him. The very first week, there was a 60-something blonde with tuna and noodles; a dyed coal-black septuagenarian with that green bean and mushroom soup recipe; and a sleek silver-haired number with her signature spaghetti. They usually bring it in a good glass casserole dish. That way the unsuspecting bachelor has to return it. Part two of the attack is getting the dish back."

Suddenly, Trish realized why Eve had been so upset with her for taking Chicken Alfredo Lasagna to Pam Brown's husband. "You don't think that Gary Brown thinks I'm one of those Casserole Ladies, do you?" Now concerned, Trish subconsciously bit her bottom lip, something that Bill had repeatedly told her to stop doing.

"Oh, honey, don't worry. Gary is probably just like my

father. These poor men don't know anything about the Casserole Ladies. They never realize what hit them until it's too late. I was just worried about you putting yourself out there and getting hurt."

Concentrating on her task, Trish didn't answer. "It's time to put your nails under the lights for a few moments."

Eve's nails looked perfect. New tips, new paint, a rhinestone cross accent on her ring finger, and now they just needed to dry. Obediently Eve placed her hands inside the nail dryer.

Trish set the timer while continuing, "Pam Brown was one of my clients for longer than you have been, Eve." The salon owner's eyes suddenly filled with tears and her voice cracked as she said, "I hate breast cancer. Whenever a woman has it, and let's face it lots of us get it, I'm the one who has to make it look like they have some hair when it's getting thin from chemotherapy. Before it all falls out or I have to shave off what remains, I'm also the one who assists them in finding the right wig, one that fits and matches their hair color."

Now Eve Hughes was the one who looked confused.

"You probably didn't know that about me, did you? I guess you could call it my ministry. I suppose I'm one of those people who go to church on Sunday, and sit in the back and never say much. Still, there's this passion inside me to help women look the very best they can while they're fighting their way through cancer."

Trish took a sip of cold coffee from her cup that was sitting on the counter. "I've always felt it was something the good Lord birthed in me. I'm pretty knowledgeable about wigs. I took some classes, so that I would be able to offer struggling ladies special assistance. We don't advertise, but there's a room in the back of the shop for cancer patients. Of course, other folks suffer hair loss, too, and I try to help them, but the reason I opened it was for women with cancer."

Eve looked at her stylist like she was seeing her for the very first time. Just then the timer went off, and Trish brightly said, "Your nails are all done."

"They look beautiful, as usual. Thanks so much, Trish." Eve was looking down admiring her nails, when suddenly she looked up into Trish's brown eyes. "Can I ask you a personal question?"

"Oh, please, we've been friends for twenty years. Shoot."

"What's it like for a woman like Pam, to lose her breasts, her hair, and then eventually her life? How do you help them?"

"I don't think Pam would mind me telling you the whole truth. She was really beautiful when she was young, and even though she was getting older like all of us, she still had gorgeous, thick red hair. We went to school together, and that hair was her trademark."

For a brief moment Trish was grief-stricken. "Her chemo made her hair fall out almost overnight. Thank God, we had ordered just the right wig a few weeks earlier. We cried together that afternoon. I didn't have any words that would take her hurt away, but I held her. She told me it was easier to lose her breasts than her hair. It's like that for some women."

"What about her husband, Gary? Was he there for her?"

"If he wouldn't have been, I would never tell you, because

it would be wrong to judge his motivation. Some men walk away because it breaks their heart into a million pieces. They can't bear not being able to fix it."

Eve handed her longtime stylist a check that included a generous tip. She never wanted to take advantage of their friendship.

"Thank you, Eve," Trish said, tucking the check in the pocket of her salon apron. "As far as Gary Brown though, the truth is I never saw a man who was kinder, more patient, or had more faith. That's why I took him the casserole. Gary really thought that his wife was going to be the one to get a miracle. Even when the doctors said there was no hope, Gary kept on believing."

"I'm surprised. I never thought he was a very compassionate person. I mean, he's a judge. You wouldn't expect a judge to be a softie."

"Don't get me wrong, Eve. I'm sure when he's Judge Gary Brown, he's a different man, but in the moments I saw him, he was Gary, the husband of a dying woman whom he loved more than his own life. I bumped into him the other day at the high school where our daughters are both seniors. He looked so thin."

"Oh, that's right, I forgot, you and Pam had your girls about the same time. Your Lexie is so gorgeous. Funny, neither of you had any other children."

Trish always enjoyed her conversations with Eve, but she realized it was time to get back to work. "Eve, you know I would love to talk to you all day, but I've got a salon to run. I have a customer coming in for a cut and color soon. I better grab my sandwich out of the refrigerator in the back. I bring a peanut butter and jelly on wheat every day. Bill would have a fit if he knew how rarely I cook since he's been gone. Don't know what I'll do when Lexie goes off to college this fall."

"Maybe I could help?" offered a middle-aged man who had just walked into Trish's manicure station. "I hope you don't mind? I told the receptionist we were old friends. Besides, she remembered me from coming in with Pam."

Trish and Eve were both startled as Gary Brown's six-foot presence filled the small space. He was the picture of professionalism in a dark blue pinstripe suit with a white shirt and burgundy silk tie. In his hands he held an old white and blue Corning Ware casserole dish.

Eve smiled a little too broadly as she stood and picked up her purse. "I'll make another appointment later, Trish. Have to get back to the office before my boss misses me." Then her face softened as she gently said to Gary, "I never had a chance to tell you how very sorry I am about your wife, Judge Brown. She was my nurse when my youngest son was born."

The attractive fifty-something man said, "Thank you, I wouldn't have made it through without good friends like Trish here."

"She is the best!" Eve agreed as she slowly turned and walked away.

She couldn't help overhearing Gary Brown say, "Thanks for the lasagna, Trish. My daughter said it was the first decent meal that she's had in months." Then he paused like he didn't know how to express what he wanted to say next. Eve also stopped in her tracks waiting for his next remark.

The judge cleared his throat. "Trish, I've never asked a woman to dinner since I met Pam thirty years ago, but I was wondering..." He hesitated again, unable to find the words.

Trish could no longer bear the suspense. "Gary, I haven't had dinner with a man other than my Bill for thirty years, either. Yet if you are asking me if I would like to have dinner with you, my answer is, 'A definite yes.'"

The judge grinned from ear to ear, like he was a schoolboy again.

But it was Eve Hughes whose cheeks blushed almost as brightly as her Fuchsia on Fire nails. On the way out of Style by Design, she mumbled to the receptionist, "I guess she's not just another Casserole Lady."

Discussion Questions for Not Just Another Casserole Lady

1) Do you feel that the friendship between Trish and Eve is a true friendship even though it began as a business relationship between a hair stylist and her client? Have you ever had a friendship begin in a similar manner?

2) Do you think Trish is genuinely naïve as Eve comes to believe or do you wonder if there might have been an ulterior motive in her taking the casserole to Gary Brown?

3) Have you had a life dream to do something that involved lots of hard work and dedication? For instance, Trish wanted to become a hairdresser and eventually owned her own salon, while her husband fulfilled his dream of becoming a veterinarian with her help. Has anyone assisted you in fulfilling your dream?

4) Do you try to financially support other individuals in their business endeavors and bless them like Eve does when she always makes sure to give Trish a generous tip?

5) Do you see Trish's salon services to customers with hair loss as a ministry, even though it is necessary for her to charge for those services to make sure that her salon remains profitable?

6) What can you do in your own life that would be considered a ministry, especially if it is not within the confines of the church walls?